The Wedding Planner's Daughter

The Wedding Planner's Daughter

Coleen Murtagh Paratore

SCHOLASTIC INC.

New York   Toronto   London   Auckland   Sydney
Mexico City   New Delhi   Hong Kong   Buenos Aires

ISBN 0-439-79808-6

12 11 10 9 8 7 6 5 4 3 2 1   5 6 7 8 9 10/0

Printed in the U.S.A.   40

First Scholastic printing, September 2005

Book design by Greg Stadnyk
The text for this book is set in Berkeley.

With love to Tony,
I'd still meet you at the altar at three.
—C. M. P.

Contents

When life throws you a pit, plant a cherry tree.

—Willa Havisham

CHAPTER 1

The Wish

Why, sometimes I've believed as many as six impossible things before breakfast.

—Lewis Carroll, *Through the Looking-Glass*

If you hear my name, Willafred, and don't picture a princess, well, hooray for you. "There's the wedding planner's daughter," they whisper. "She's nothing like her mother."

My mother, Stella Havisham, is as glamorous as a queen. I'm string-bean skinny with horse-tail hair. My eyes are nice, though. Blue, like the sea.

We moved here to the sea last year. Bramble, Cape Cod, where Mother was born. So far we've lived in seven towns. We move when Stella gets scared. But Nana kept on begging her "stubborn as seaweed" daughter to come home, and at last Stella agreed.

After all those years, when Stella finally said yes, well, that gave me hope for impossible things. Now Nana says, "Let's pray Stella catches a fisherman."

I love Cape Cod. I'll never forget the day we drove across that roller-coaster bridge, whitecaps sparkling on the waves below. I opened the window and the wind whooshed in and wrapped around me. *Welcome, Willa, welcome home.*

Right then I had this feeling my dream could happen here.

I hope you have better luck wishing than me. You know on your birthday when the cake comes and you close your eyes into that dark, magical moment, and then you take a leapfrog leap of faith and make that one extra-special, all-important, pretty-please, now-or-never-or-forever-hold-your-peace *wish*?

Well, if there's a secret to it, send me a postcard. I've wished the very same wish every single year, but it never, ever comes true.

I'm hoping thirteen will be my lucky birthday, though. And so, while I'm hiding up here in the choir loft, spying on Stella's rehearsal, eating cherry cordials and reading *Tom Sawyer,* watching Mrs.

Bellimo belch out "Ave Maria" like she's debuting at Carnegie Hall, and even though it's only May and my birthday's not for eight months yet, I'm believing in impossible things.

I looked it up on the calendar, and my birthday will be on a Friday. Friday the thirteenth. So, who cares? Whoop-de-do. Maybe I'll have reverse luck. Maybe I'll give Friday the thirteenth a whole new reputation.

Maybe this will be the birthday. Maybe Bramble will be the place. Maybe, finally, I'll get a father.

CHAPTER 2

The Rules

She makes me wash, they comb me all to thunder;
she won't let me sleep in the woodshed. . . . The
widder [widow] eats by a bell; she goes to bed by
a bell; she gits up by a bell—everything's so awful
reg'lar a body can't stand it.

—Mark Twain, *The Adventures of Tom Sawyer*

I rush in from school, past the locked entrance
to Mother's studio, Weddings by Havisham, and
run two steps at a time up to the second floor.

The building was formerly Bramble Funeral
Home. They had the funerals on the first floor,
they embalmed the bodies in the basement (not
that I want to creep you out or anything), and the
funeral director's family lived on the second floor,
where we do now.

Stella is looking out the window in the study.

The drapes are parted ever so slightly so no one will see her watching. Stella is so absorbed in what she's doing that she doesn't even realize I'm here.

Now, your family might call a room like this the family room or the den, but believe me, in our home the study deserves its name. This is where Mother waits for my after-school arrival, poised and ready for battle.

Stella's head is moving slowly in a circular motion. I nearly shout with excitement because I know who she is watching and it fits beautifully into my plans. I step back quietly, but Stella's radar has resumed. "That man is a fool," she pronounces, pulling the drape closed and neatly tucking a stray black lock into her tight French twist. "You have a science quiz tomorrow, don't you, Willafred?"

"Mother, please call me Willa. Please? Tina calls me Willa. She says it sounds like *willow,* as in willow tree, and that's much more glamorous than Willafred."

Tina Belle has a movie-star face and wispy angel hair. She's so pretty she glitters. And she's the closest I've ever come to a best friend.

"Yes, exactly." Mother's chin rises. "Which is why you, Willafred Havisham, won't hear me calling

Willa to dinner at six. We both know what glamour gets in the way of, don't we?" That would be Rule #4: Glamour gets in the way of greatness.

I roll my eyes behind her back. "Mother, could we please eat early tonight? I've got a game. We're playing Eastham, and Coach is letting me play forward. And I finished all my homework at school."

Mother's chin, which is my barometer of weather to come, swings swiftly toward the North Pole. A battle is brewing. I can sympathize with old Tom Sawyer. Thanks to Widow Stella and the rules, everything is "awful reg'lar" around here, too.

Mother has "great expectations" for me to get into a "top college" and have a "rewarding career" (although obviously not as a wedding planner, since she won't let me near the weddings), and she thinks a rule book the size of a Bible will make all that happen.

The brave knights begin. *En garde.* Stella leads.

"History?"

"Check."

"Science?"

"Done."

"Math?"

"Here's proof." (This is sort of fun.)

"Social studies?"

"Finished."

"English?"

"Need you ask?"

"Art? Music?"

"Yes." (Whoop-de-do, could be I'm free at last.)

But then Sir Stella strikes a blow, *directement à mon coeur,* straight to my heart. *"Avez-vous étudié pour votre essai français le mardi prochain?"*

I'm melting, I'm melting. No, I haven't studied for next Tuesday's French test. I just broke Rule #3: Homework is never finished. You should study for every possible exam, test, review, and planned or unplanned pop quiz that may or may never occur tomorrow, next week, next month, or next year, because what matters is the knowledge gained, and you can never have too much knowledge. Here are some other rules:

#1: Girls should have great expectations.

#2: Don't count on Prince Charming; he could fall off his horse.

#5: Lights out by nine o'clock on school nights.

#6: Stay away from the studio.

#7: STAY AWAY FROM WEDDINGS.

And the list goes on and on.

After dinner and dishes I change into my soccer uniform. I pick up the photograph of Father on my dresser and stare at his dark blue eyes. Then I see mine in the mirror. No wonder it makes Mother sad to look at me.

I wish Father could be here to take me to the game. I bet he'd cheer louder than anybody. I bet he'd come to my practices, too, and kick a ball with me in the backyard until the lightning bugs came out, French test or not. I wonder if the Poet, next door, plays soccer? Stella's not big on team sports. She runs five miles every morning, alone.

Mother drives me to the field. "Here you go," she says. "It's over at seven thirty, right?"

"Yep. Watch me, okay?"

All the other parents bring lawn chairs to the games. They clap and shout advice and plan sleepover parties for their kids. Stella usually stays in the car doing paperwork.

Eastham's a tough team. I'm nervous playing forward. Coach finally gave me a chance. We're down one with two minutes left when I spot an opening and slam in a lefty. Score! The field erupts with excitement, and all the Bramble Bees come shrieking toward me. Heart pounding, I quickly search the happy faces on the sidelines.

Stella's leaning against the car, facing away, talking on her cell phone.

That night I see Mother at the study window again. She's looking down at the Poet's backyard labyrinth. Her head is tracing its circular shape in the air. Perfect.

It's after ten. I'm breaking Rule #5. This is one of the hardest rules for me because I love to read. My favorite novels and books of poetry are here on my nightstand for whenever I need them. Certain lines make me happy. Certain characters are like friends. All these years, moving from town to town, it's been hard to make real friends.

Tonight I'm rereading *Little House in the Big Woods,* by Laura Ingalls Wilder, a favorite since I was little. The father in the story is so kind to his daughters, Laura and Mary, and he has blue eyes just like my father. . . .

"Willafred! It's a school night!"

"Sorry, Mother." I shut off the light. "Good night."

CHAPTER 3

Cherry Cordials

When I saw you by the trees of cherry,
I knew you were the one I'd marry.

—Billy Havisham

My father was a man with big, crazy ideas who liked to write poetry. I wish I could have met him, but he died before I was born. When I was younger, Mother refused to talk about how they met, or about their wedding day, or about the horrible tragedy that happened the very next day, but when I'd come to Cape Cod for summer vacations with Nana, she would tell me the stories again and again, until I could picture it in my mind.

Now I've replayed the movie so many times I'm not sure exactly which parts are fact and which are fiction, but it's my movie, so whoop-de-do.

Estelle Clancy and Billy Havisham met one fine

spring in Washington, D.C. Mother had just finished her M.B.A. and was taking a vacation before wowing Wall Street. "Stella graduated top of her class," Nana said. "She was going to be a big-shot businesswoman. She had no intention of being swept off her feet by some sweet-talking man."

My father, William Frederick "Call Me Billy" Havisham, ran an advertising agency in Washington called What's the Big Idea? Billy was jogging through Poet's Park on his lunch hour when the wind whooshed, *wait*, and he turned just in time to see this beautiful woman strolling toward him through a fog of pink and white.

Pink and white cherry blossoms. At first Billy thought he was dreaming, but Stella was the real deal. In an instant Billy fell head over sneakers in love. Good thing for him, Stella did too. Although she was probably wearing sandals.

It was springtime in Washington, when the cherry blossoms bloom. When the ripe, sweet scent of cherry perfume makes strangers babble like bobolinks. Mother was so smitten with love she canceled her Wall Street job interviews and extended her vacation. Nana said Stella's "beef-tough business brain" softened with every sweet sonnet Billy composed for her in Poet's Park. After a whirlwind romance they got engaged.

"Billy was the boy for Stella," Nana said. "Even as a little girl she was always too serious for her own good. Billy made her giggle."

Mother giggling? I still can't imagine that.

Much to Nana's dismay, Stella decided the wedding would be in Washington, since that's where she and Billy had met. "If the truth be told," said Nana, "I think Stella thought Cape Cod was too quaint and old-fashioned for her sophisticated plans."

Shortly after their engagement Billy "crossed the pond" to open up branches of the Big Idea in London, Paris, and Brussels. Once a week he sent Stella a poem and a box of cordials, chocolate-covered cherries, as a token of his love. Listen to this one:

When I saw you by the trees of cherry,
I knew you were the one I'd marry.

Could that man write or what?

Meanwhile, back here in the States, in between sniffling over the poems and chomping on the chocolates, Stella had a mission. To plan the perfect wedding.

All by herself. Which wasn't too big of a problem, since she didn't have meddling older sisters or know-it-all grandmothers or a henhouse of great-aunts and third cousins cackling about, insisting they were experts on gowns and flowers. And Father was an orphan, so there wasn't a posse of in-laws pining to put their two pennies in.

Nana offered to close her store, Clancy's Candy, and come to Washington to help, but no, Stella would oversee every detail herself. And believe me, you don't mess with Mother when she's on a mission.

"Stella became obsessed with creating the perfect wedding," Nana said.

I can see Mother reading tons of books on wedding planning. Devouring countless magazines. I can see Stella sleuthing around synagogues and chapels; dancing into country clubs and banquet halls; stalking chic designer showrooms, beauty salons, bakeries, florists, and caterers; snapping photographs; filling notebooks; studying weddings like you study for a college degree.

Stella didn't stop until she had what she needed:

the twelve ingredients for a perfect wedding.

Meanwhile, Billy's business boomed. "He kept sending Stella the names of new European friends to invite," Nana said. "Billy was a charmer. Everybody loved him."

Sure enough, the wedding of Estelle Marie Clancy and William Frederick Havisham was a work of art. One newspaper clipping Nana showed me compared it to the wedding of Prince Charles and Lady Diana. It was that perfectly perfect.

My parents married in the springtime, when the cherry blossoms bloomed. After a breathtaking ceremony at the National Cathedral a hundred white doves were released in the air. A regal carriage with four black stallions in full-dress plumage whisked the newlyweds off to the posh Crowne Plaza Hotel, where hundreds of adoring guests awaited their arrival in the Grand Ballroom.

The jubilant couple toasted with the finest French champagne. They dined on beluga caviar and foie gras and Cornish hens (they had to have lots of fancy European food, since so many guests were from across the pond). The bride and groom waltzed until the clock struck midnight. Then they followed a path of cherry blossoms to their honeymoon suite, whereupon William recited his wedding poem to Estelle as moonbeams danced off the teardrop chandelier and twinkled like stars in her ebony hair. . . . (Okay, so I'm going overboard with the movie, but really, it could have happened that way.)

Then, in the morning, Stella awoke to a silver tea tray with warm scones and jam, a single cherry blossom in a crystal vase, and a note. Being a man of big ideas, Billy had dreamed up a dramatic surprise for his new wife. "Meet me in Poet's Park at noon."

I imagine Mother laughing, wiping away a tear, thinking, *What a wonderfully charming cad I've married. I can't wait to have tons of wonderfully charming children, beginning with a wonderfully charming daughter named Willa who will have blue eyes just like his.* (Okay, so I'm stretching the taffy here.)

A white limousine carried Stella to the park in style, her six red leather trunks in tow. Now, this is where the story gets a little fuzzy.

Stella sat waiting on their favorite bench in Poet's Park, basking in the sunlight, smiling at squirrels, awaiting her beloved's arrival. One hour.

Two hours. Three hours passed by. In a time before people had phones in their pockets. *Where is he? Where is he?* On and on and on she waited.

As nightfall neared and it got chilly a police officer noticed beautiful Stella sitting there, looking frozen, stiff as stone. A pigeon was perched on her shoulder. The six red trunks, filled with exquisite honeymoon outfits, sat beside her, buried beneath a snowy layer of cherry blossoms.

Gently the officer tapped Stella's arm. "Madame, who are you waiting for?"

Stella's brown eyes moved upward slowly, blinking as if awakening from a dream. Again, the kind officer repeated his question, this time in a louder voice.

"Madame, who are you waiting for?"

That's when the statue cracked and rivers of tears flowed.

The New York and Washington papers covered the tragedy with dignity. The tabloids were less kind: AMATEUR HOT-AIR BALLOONIST BATTLES WITH BIRDS AND SINKS. The *Cape Cod Times* quoted a Bramble local: "Stella Clancy's charming Billy took a final dip in the pond that day."

Well, at least I'm not a complete orphan. At

least I still have Mother. And I do feel really sorry about what happened, but it's been almost thirteen years, and I know Father would understand if Mother got married again. He'd want her to be happy.

He'd want *me* to be happy.

CHAPTER 4

The Poet

There is no Frigate like a Book
To take us Lands away
Nor any Coursers like a Page
Of prancing Poetry.

—Emily Dickinson

Stella and I have been on the two-year plan. Just about every two years, just when I'm starting to feel safe and settled and close to getting a best friend, Mother gets that dreaded statue-face look and says: "Willafred, it's time for the trunks." It's not that she heads toward anything better, just away from what she's afraid of.

Stella never has trouble finding customers. When she hangs the sign WEDDINGS BY HAVISHAM and opens her studio gallery with the twelve signature easels, people start talking. Then all it takes is one wedding, and she has more business than she can handle.

If you've got a map, you can plot our route up the eastern seaboard from Washington, D.C., where I was born. First to Baltimore, then Philadelphia, then Newark, Hartford, Providence, and now Bramble, Cape Cod, state of Massachusetts. I sure hope the road ends here. The Cape is a peninsula. Next stop is the Atlantic Ocean.

Now, unless you're a nomad, Gypsy, or some other roving rogue, I think you can appreciate that it's not exactly a barrel of laughs starting over— "Who's THAT?"—at a brand-new school every two years. The only thing that fits that barrel analogy is that you do start to feel like a monkey. *Hee-hee-hee-hee-hee-hee-hee-hee-who's-THAT?*

It's been getting even harder now that I'm nearly a teenager. Now when we move into a new town, all the girls have their club membership rosters engraved in gold and nailed on the front door of school. Sometimes in those first few weeks in a new place the only friends I have are the ones in my books. They never let me down.

But things are looking better in Bramble. Tina and I are getting close, Nana lets me work at

Clancy's Candy, and Mr. Tweed, the owner of Bramblebriar Books, is a real kindred spirit. Sulamina Mum is wonderful, and of course there's Joseph Francis Kennelly. He's so cute.

It never gets me anywhere to complain about moving. Besides, it takes me time to size up a new town and figure out whether there's an eligible man for my mother. No husband for my mother, no father for me. You don't need a calculator to do the math.

There have been a lot of nice guys, but none was a match for Stella, with her steely suit of armor. Nana says, "He's going to have to sweep her up quick and whisk her away before she has time to think about it."

Stella does date. She'll go out to dinner or a movie with a guy a few times, but if she senses he's starting to get serious, it's all over. And if a guy is ever foolish enough to try some sweet, old-fashioned romance, he's dead in the water. One time this handsome guy, Zane Friday, was so smitten with Stella he brought musicians and serenaded her with a love song beneath her bedroom window. Like something out of *Romeo and Juliet*. Zane sang with such passion his face turned hot-pepper red.

Stella cooled him off with a bucket of water.

I've got high hopes for the Poet, though. That would be "the fool" Mother was watching from the study window. Sam Gracemore. Isn't that a lovely name?

Just a few weeks after we moved to Bramble last summer, Sam moved in next door. Our fancy brick house feels cold and formal. The lawn is always freshly mowed, the hedges evenly trimmed. The Poet's big white house needs a bath. A broken green shutter hangs sideways like it's waving. The stone fence is crumbling down.

Nana says Sam's house was once the elegant Bramblebriar Inn. Generations of Gracemores lived there. It's been abandoned for nearly a decade, though, ever since Sam's grandmother Rose died. Much to the family's surprise, she willed the place to Sam. She said it was because he loved the sea the most.

The Poet's house has several chimneys and a rooftop porch called a widow's walk. That's a popular Cape thing, a widow's walk. Long ago women would pace back and forth up there, gazing out to sea, hoping to spot their husband's ship. But the sailing life was treacherous, many men never came home; thus the name widow's walk.

I spotted the Poet the day he moved in. It was a muggy August morning, and I was sitting by the study window previewing the seventh-grade math textbook, Stella's idea of summer school, when I looked out and saw a man putting a sign on the lawn next door. I called Mother, and she put down her stock report and came to the window to see.

"Good," she said. "Maybe he's having a tag sale. Hopefully he'll get that dump into shape. The grass hasn't been mowed in ten years."

That afternoon Mother and I passed by the sign on our way into town for school supplies.

Go confidently in the direction of your dreams.
—Henry David Thoreau

Ooh, nice, he likes poetry, I thought.

Mother rolled her eyes and made her disappointed-with-the-ineptness-of-humanity huffing sound. Later, when we returned from town, the Poet was sweeping his front porch. He smiled and waved. Such a handsome man. I looked to see if Mother had noticed. "Hello," Mother said quickly, and kept walking. Yes, she had noticed.

"Can't we at least stop and meet him?" I whispered. Never mind bring our new neighbor a plate of brownies or invite him for a picnic on Sunday. Stella would never make it as a member of the Bramble Welcome Wagon.

"No," Mother said. "Let's get your backpack ready for school."

Then the very next night Mother and I walked into the Open House at Bramble Academy, and there was Sam Gracemore, standing with the faculty. The Poet was going to be my English teacher! Talk about luck. When Sam saw us, he smiled.

The line moved slowly, but when we finally reached the Poet, he and Stella shook hands and forgot to let go. You could almost see a lightning bolt zap between them.

Instantly I hulked into a fullback to block the advancing line of people behind us. *Keep talking, Mother. Keep talking.* And they did. The Poet leaned down to say something and Mother smiled. Then Mother tilted upward to say something and the Poet smiled. The gym was stifling and noisy, but Stella and Sam were someplace else. Someplace nicer. Oblivious to the face-making, eye-rolling line of people.

But then a lady with purple eye shadow and clown red lips coughed loudly and broke the spell. I later found out she was that obnoxious Ruby Snivler's mother. Ruby used to be Tina's best friend. The Poet craned his neck to keep talking, but Mother had already moved on to Mr. Mistletoe, the music teacher with halitosis.

As we made our way down the row of teachers I knew Stella was donning her suit of armor, forcing herself not to look back. But I also knew that the Poet's sunny smile had melted an itsy icicle-size path into Stella's frozen heart. And from that evening on, at every Bramble Academy function, from Harvest Dinner to Math Counts to Readers and Writers Rule, whenever the Poet and Mother were in the same room, it felt like somebody had turned the thermostat up. Now I just needed to get them on a date.

CHAPTER 5

The Twelve Perfect Ingredients

Something old, something new,
Something borrowed, something blue,
And a lucky sixpence in her shoe.

—Anonymous

"Shhh!" I warn Tina as we sneak downstairs. It's past eleven on a Friday night and Tina's sleeping over. So far everything is going great, but Tina's so excited to see inside Weddings by Havisham, I'm afraid she'll wake Mother.

"Shhh!" I turn the key and open the forbidden door, breaking Rule #6, Stay away from the studio, once again. I always come the night before one of Mother's weddings. I bring scissors, a needle, thread, and the thirteenth secret ingredient, all stuffed in Mother's old satin wedding purse, once white, now beige with age.

Mother doesn't realize it, but I'm the secret to her wedding-planning success. Ever since I started adding the thirteenth secret ingredient, her success has skyrocketed.

It was in Hartford that I discovered the other reason why we kept moving every couple of years. I used to think it was only because Mother didn't want to get too attached to a man who might potentially break her heart again. But then, one day, I heard Mrs. DeNucci and the others talking at Candi's Cut Above.

My dryer had clicked off and my hairdresser, Kimmy, hadn't noticed. Right away I knew something was wrong. All the ladies were shaking their heads with expressions of disbelief, as if discussing the most dreadful news. And they were all looking at me.

I kept my eyes glued on *Glamour* magazine. They didn't realize I could hear.

"It must have been the wedding planner," Mrs. DeNucci said, her voice rising, nearly toppling out of her seat with the sheer enormity of her distress.

"She jinxed my daughter, that woman did. The

wedding was perfect, beautiful, no one's saying anything about that, but the very next day my Joanie broke down sobbing like a crazy person, *pazzo*, bizarro, like she was possessed."

"YES!" Mrs. Fox shrieked, frantically pushing perm foils away from her ears. "That's the same thing that happened to my Allison. Ms. Havisham planned her wedding, too! Just like you said, Mrs. DeNucci, it was a gorgeous wedding, soup to nuts, but the next day Allison started crying and couldn't stop. It was like someone put a *spell* on her."

Shock shook the salon. Kimmy collapsed. Washers, cutters, stylists, and curlers stopped washing, cutting, styling, and curling. Then they all turned and stared at me.

"Oh, how glam!" Tina is squealing, and I snap back.

With a flip of the switch Tina has illuminated the wedding planner's latest creation. Tina is slowly panning the room like a movie camera operator, trying to capture every detail. "Wow," she says. "It's beautiful."

There are many beautiful things to see, but if you ever saw Stella's studio, it's the easels you'd remember. Twelve of them, in a circle around the room, each one covered with a red velvet curtain. I flick another switch and the spotlights turn on. One light aimed on each red-draped easel, like paintings in a gallery.

It is the night before the wedding of Alabaster "Allie" Granite and Bartholomew "Bart" Vador. Tina and I walk slowly around the circle. She squeals as I pull on each gold cord and the curtains part to reveal the subject underneath. Each easel displays a photograph or final sketch of one of the wedding planner's Twelve Perfect Ingredients: The gown. The tuxedo and bridal party ensemble. The invitation. The ceremony. The reception (in this case a photograph of the terrace of Ballymar Country Club, set up as it will look tomorrow). The flowers. The menu. The table settings and favors. The music. The photographer. The cake. The limousine.

"Just gorgeous," says Tina. She's looking at Alabaster Granite's wedding gown, glowing as if lit from within. Tina doesn't know this, but according to the wedding planner's explicit instructions, someone from the bride's family will come promptly at 8:00 A.M. tomorrow to pick up the gown. Stella does not leave anything to chance, and if the dress remains in her possession until the big day, nothing will harm it. No wrinkle or speck of the unexpected will sully the wedding gown. The First Perfect Ingredient.

Each of the twelve ingredients is exquisite. Together tomorrow they will form a masterpiece. The wedding of Alabaster Granite and Bartholomew Vador will be an original work of art, unlike any other. Ms. Havisham has made certain of that. It is her expertise.

"Ooooooh," Tina coos. "This is going to be even more beautiful than Duke and Dora's wedding in Tahiti." Tina looks like she might faint.

"Wow," I say, giving Tina a cherry cordial to stabilize her. You never know just when a cordial is going to come in handy. "Better than Duke and Dora's? Really?" This is just about the highest compliment that Tina Belle can bestow. Duke and Dora are her favorite characters on her favorite daytime drama, *Forever Young*. Tina tapes the episodes she misses and watches them on the twenty-inch TV in her room at night. I've seen it only once or twice. We don't watch much television. Stella says it's a "brain drain." And we especially don't watch sappy romances or, gosh forbid, shhhh, *beauty pageants*. Mother can't even mention those without getting a migraine.

"Knock, knock? Willa? Anybody there?" Tina shakes me back to the present as I walk her home the next day. Mother is already off to the Granite-Vador wedding.

"I said maybe you could sleep over at my house next Friday."

Two sleepovers in a row? Sounds like best friends to me. "Sure, great. I'll ask."

Then Tina says, "I'll invite Ruby, too. Let's do a beauty night. I'll borrow my mom's manicure stuff, and maybe Ruby can bring her aunt Philly's wedding album. Ruby was a junior bridesmaid, you know."

"Yes, I know. Sure, whatever." Why does the Snivler have to come? Cherries are churning in my stomach. I ate way too many more cordials after Tina finally fell asleep at 2:00 A.M. and I sneaked back downstairs to add the thirteenth secret ingredient to the wedding planner's masterpiece.

CHAPTER 6

The Wedding Planner

*A book? . . . What d'you want a flaming book for? . . .
We've got a lovely telly with a twelve-inch screen
and now you come asking for a book!*

—Roald Dahl, *Matilda*

At the start all the girls at Bramble Academy
wanted to be my friend. They probably thought it
would be exciting to hang out at my house, watching the wedding planner wave her magical wedding wand.

But it didn't take long for word to get out: The
wedding planner's daughter is not allowed anywhere near the wedding planner's studio.

I've got that big-toothed Ruby Snivler in my
class to thank for that. Actually, it's Sivler, but I

think Snivler suits her better. Remember, her mother was the cougher at open house who broke the bolt between Sam and Stella. That whole family is annoying.

Anyway, Ruby Snivler was a junior bridesmaid in her aunt Philly Cheeseface's (actually, it's Cheeseborough's) wedding, the first wedding Mother planned in Bramble. Since Ruby was a classmate, I thought Mother would make an exception to Rule #6, but when I appeared at the studio door, Mother shouted, "Up to the study, Willafred!"

Well, Snivler's juicy jaws couldn't wait to chatter like a chimp to all the girls in her club, which with my sorry luck was the biggest and best club in the class. Actually, it's the only club; there are only ten girls in the whole class. "Guess what? The wedding planner's daughter can't go near the weddings!"

I bet bees buzzed overtime in Bramble with that one. They all probably figured I was a freak who somehow ruined weddings, and so my mother, the famous wedding planner, had banned me to life in the study, like some sort of Quasimodo.

But as much as I resent Stella for keeping me

out of her life, believe it or not, she does have a good reason. Heartbroken with sadness over the hot-air balloon death of her beloved Billy, Stella's rivers of tears soon froze. *Why had he been so foolish? Couldn't we have just hailed a taxi to the airport like normal people heading off on their honeymoon? If he hadn't been such a prattle-brained romantic, he'd still be here. . . .*

Filled with anger at having her fairy-tale life swept away by the wind, literally, and filled with too much pride to slink back home to Nana after she'd turned her back on Bramble, and throwing up every morning with morning sickness because she was [newly] pregnant with me, Stella made a decision.

She would take care of herself and her baby on her own. No more husbands for her. She hadn't needed a man before, and she didn't need one now. She had her M.B.A. She'd need a good income to support us, and Stella knew that the Daddy Warbucks–size bucks were in running your own business. But what kind?

Knowing Mother's fondness for homework, I bet she headed straight to the library and pored through tons of books. I imagine the one entitled

What Color Is Your Parachute? gave her heartburn, after the whole hot-air balloon fiasco, but I bet a lightbulb went off when one book asked: "What do you know a lot about? Are you an expert at something?" *Ding.* Stella buzzed in first on that *Jeopardy!* question.

Weddings. She was an expert at planning weddings.

Now, I'm kind of fuzzy on this next part, but let's see if we can connect the dots. Six months after Stella decided to become a wedding planner, she took a taxi to the hospital in the dead of winter, all alone, writhing in pain, ready to deliver her baby (me).

And on January 13 at 10:03 P.M., when the nurse wiped that darling little screaming, red-faced cherub (me) and wrapped that little package in an adorable blanket and handed it (me) to the stunningly beautiful woman in the bed, Stella looked in my blue eyes and cried. The resemblance to Father was striking.

"A name, dear?" the nurse asked kindly.

"Willafred," Mother whispered. "Willafred Clancy Havisham."

I bet the nurse wrote it down, thinking, *Oh,*

poor baby, what a name. I hope they at least nick-name her Willa, which sounds like willow *and is so much more glamorous.*

Later that night Stella made two solemn vows. The first was that other than the *Will* from *William* and the *fred* from *Frederick,* I would inherit nothing from my father. Stella would slam that castle door and throw away the key.

Her daughter, Willafred, would not become a literally lost-in-the-clouds dreamer like Billy had been. Willafred would not spend her life waiting for Prince Charming. Willafred, who would never be nicknamed Willa because that might sound like *willow tree* and be far too glamorous for greatness, this girl, Willafred, would learn to take care of herself. She would be strong and serious and smart. She would not set her sights on some dashing, hot-air-filled cad of a poet whisking her off in a balloon someday. Because as anyone with half a good business brain knows, balloons pop.

The second solemn vow Mother made that night was that her daughter would never be allowed near her while she did her wedding planner work. Stella didn't want dreams of gowns and grooms stealing brain cells away from studying.

Because as we all know from Rule #4, glamour gets in the way of greatness.

Stella, of course, despite being gorgeous and glamorous, has certainly achieved greatness. She's the closest Bramble's ever come to a celebrity. And all the businesses in town are hoping she'll bring some real celebrity weddings here. Framed articles about Stella in *Bride's Day, Wedding Bliss,* and *Fortune* line her office walls like diplomas. Stella starts her day with the *Wall Street Journal* and snuggles up with *Barron's* business magazine at night. No romance novels for Stella, uh-uh. She never reads fiction. Last year I bought her a book of poetry by Emily Dickinson, but that has disappeared.

Mother once liked poems, though. The poems Father wrote for her. She even wrote some for him. I found them in the heart.

I was about eight years old when I first discovered Stella's heart. Scary noises woke me up in the middle of the night—trees creaking, wind howling, the first big snowstorm of the season. Down the hallway I saw the light on in Mother's room, the door slightly ajar. As I walked closer the sound grew louder. I looked in and saw Mother kneeling on the rug with a red box.

Now, I am quite familiar with Mother's red trunks. We haul them out and pack them up every couple of years when Stella gets that statue look. But this red trunk was smaller than the others and oddly shaped, like a heart.

In one hand Mother clutched a piece of paper. A letter perhaps? Her other hand was clamped over her mouth, trying to muffle the sobs that shook her body as she rocked back and forth. Mother looked so sad, so helpless, I wanted to rush in and hug her, but I knew she'd be angry. I lay awake for hours thinking about what I had seen.

Luckily, the next day Mr. Puffis had to have an emergency root canal and canceled our piano lessons, so I got home early. I listened at the door of Mother's studio, and when I heard her say, "No, Mrs. Pisarski, I'm sorry, but there will be no pink carnations in one of my weddings. I understand they have a certain sentimental value, since that's what you carried in your bouquet two decades ago, but pink carnations are simply not original enough for your daughter," I knew Stella was explaining the Sixth Perfect Ingredient to her newest client and that I had some time to snoop.

Mother's bedroom in every house we've ever lived in is always impeccably neat. No wrinkles on the spread, no socks in the corner, no dust bunnies hopping along the dresser. It took me a few minutes, but finally I found it. There at the far back of Mother's closet, behind the cottons and linens safely hibernating through the winter until they might fashionably reawaken and move about in the spring, there was the red heart.

I picked it up, light as a feather, and carried it out to the rug by Mother's bed. My hands trembled as I lifted the gold latch. The memory of Mother sitting there sobbing the night before swirled into my mind like a ghost.

And while that is an image I'll never forget, it is not what I remember most about that night. What I remember most is that Mother was wearing her wedding gown.

CHAPTER 7

Bramble

If you're fond of sand dunes and salty air,
Quaint little villages here and there,
You're sure to fall in love with Old Cape Cod.
— From the song "Old Cape Cod"

After leaving Tina's house, I hear the bells at BUC, Bramble United Congregational, and rush down Main Street to sneak a peak at Allie Granite and Bart Vador's wedding. A mile from the water the sea air still flutters against my face like a butterfly. Bramble is a magical place. There's a feeling of history. I can almost hear voices from centuries ago rising up from the cobblestone streets. There's a feeling of future here too. It's in the laughter and spirit of anticipation that each new tourist brings.

Bramble was once a seaport village, home of the famous nineteenth-century whaler Mitticus J.

Bramble. The stately houses, some with brass plaques stating BUILT IN 1864 or NATIONAL REGISTER OF HISTORIC PLACES, are red brick or white clapboard with black or green shutters. Bramble United Congregational, where my friend Sulamina Mum is minister, stands at attention at one end of Main Street, and the ivy-covered Bramble Free Library salutes back from the other. Snuggled in between are restaurants and clothing shops, a two-screen cinema, hardware store, florist, card shop, fish market, pharmacy, two art galleries, a few tacky gift shops, and my two favorite places of all: Clancy's Candy and Bramblebriar Books.

Lucky for me, Nana understands the importance of cherry cordials to my daily constitution. I stop by every Friday to pick up my box. It's one of our little secrets. Stella would be mad if she knew. Nana makes the very best kind of cordials. Fresh cherries, with the pits still in for luck, swimming in cherry syrup, covered with rich milk chocolate. I save the pits. They're seeds, you know, that can blossom into cherry trees.

I open the door to Clancy's and dive into a sugary sea. Waves of chocolate, vanilla, and peppermint float up to greet me. Nana smiles and says,

"Give me a hug, shmug," always so happy to see me. Nana's been alone since Grandpa died. He was the love of her life. Her scruffy little black-and-white dog, Scamp, slobbers me with kisses, then he lies on his back, sticks his four paws up, and looks at me, *Well, what are you waiting for, Willa, are you going to rub my stomach or what?* I swear that dog talks.

Whenever I can get away from the study for a while, Nana pays me to help her. Minimum wage plus free candy. Stella doesn't believe in big allowances, so I appreciate the money. And it's fun. I cut the pans of fudge into neat squares and refill the penny candy bins. My most important job is to remind kids to use the shovels to scoop the Swedish fish. It drives Nana crazy when kids stick "grubby paws" in her fish.

I'm also Nana's chief saltwater taffy tester. Cape Cod is famous for its saltwater taffy, and Nana's trying to create the best new flavor on Cape. (That's what we locals say, not "on *the* Cape," just "on Cape.") Every year *Cape Cod Life* magazine does the "Best Of" issue, and Nana wants to win for Best Sweets on the Upper Cape. She keeps experimenting with new flavors. So far it's been hit-and-miss. She thought she was clever with the clam chowder one, but hey, who wants fish for dessert?

While we work, Nana and I plot ways to get Mother married. When we first moved here, Nana had a hunky Mashpee fisherman in mind, but then she met the Poet on Grandparents' Day at Bramble Academy. "That's the sailor for Stella," she said with a wink. "Let's keep the compass coined on him." Actually, I think she overheard me and Sam talking about poetry and realized he would be a perfect father for me.

When I leave the cozy comfort of Clancy's Candy, I walk two doors down to Bramblebriar Books, where my friend Mr. Tweed never disappoints me either. When the door bells jingle, he comes out from the back room, sometimes with a limp, "that old arthritis again," and shakes my hand. "Willa, hello. So glad you came." Then he makes us a pot of lemon tea. No milk, no sugar. That's the way we take our tea.

We sit on the couch with our feet on the ottoman, sipping tea and talking about books. Mr. Tweed says to read lots of good books now because you might get too busy when you grow up. When

I get up to leave, Mr. Tweed says, "Muffles is keeping it warm." I walk to the window ledge and scratch the gray cat's fluffy coat. She leaps and I retrieve my treasure. A book, chosen especially by Mr. Tweed, a man who understands the importance of books to my daily constitution.

I'm keeping a list of my favorites. I call it "Willa's Pix." I got the idea from Tina. When the Belles went to that famous Saratoga racetrack in New York last August, Tina got a tip sheet called "Kids' Pix." Local kids pick out horses they think are winners. The Belles stayed in a fancy hotel where ballerinas from the New York City Ballet sipped lemonade by a fountain in the garden. Doesn't that sound glamorous?

It's three o'clock. Right about now the organist's hands are hovering over the keys at our church, BUC. Mrs. Bellimo, in a flowered hat, clears her throat and rests her gloved hand on the organ for support. The guests rise, adjust jackets, smooth dresses, their tissues and cameras in hand, jockeying for position. Alabaster Granite stands in the wings with her father, confident of the wedding planner's Twelve Perfect Ingredients, unaware of the secret thirteenth ingredient I added late last night. Bart Vador, stunning in his black tuxedo, shuffles nervously at the altar.

They all wait, frozen in time. They wait for Ms. Havisham's cue. At her signal, and hers alone, the bride will begin processing. One, two, look right, nod. One, two, look left, smile. Just as the wedding planner has instructed. I'm watching the whole movie in my mind as I turn the corner and walk smack into the Poet.

CHAPTER 8

A Suitor to Suit Her

Whoever is happy will make others happy too.
—*Anne Frank: The Diary of a Young Girl*

"Willa, hello! Fancy running into you."

Somebody ought to paint a picture of the Poet's smile. It sort of stays with you like that Mona Lisa lady's. I'm amazed at my luck. I never have a chance to tell Sam to ask Stella for a date when we're talking about grammar or Shakespeare at school.

"I was listening to the bells, Mr. Gracemore. That's one of Mother's weddings."

"Please call me Sam outside of class, Willa. 'Mr. Gracemore' is too formal for neighbors. Yes, I understand she has quite a talent. Your mother, that is."

A gaggle of seagulls honk by like alarm bells

and we look up. *Caw, caw, caw.* The Poet awk-
wardly stuffs his hands into the pockets of his
jeans. A black thread hangs from a button on his
light blue denim shirt. He probably didn't have
light blue thread.

I feel sorry for Sam. Nana found out he lost his
wife and son in a car crash ten years ago. Maggie
and two-year-old Robbie had been out shopping
for Sam's birthday when a truck swerved and they
were forced off a cliff. The yellow balloons Robbie
had picked out special for his daddy floated up
into the clouds.

"How do you get over a tragedy like that?"
Nana had said, shaking her head. "Imagine losing
your wife and only child all in one day."

I remember thinking, *Mother lost Father, but at
least she still has me.*

When the Poet's story got around Bramble,
everyone expected he'd be a sad, bitter man. But
Sam surprised them by bringing his grandmother
Gracemore's backyard labyrinth back to life and
putting a word board on his front lawn. People in
town feel so badly about his loss that nobody,
except Stella of course, complains about the sign.
Most people actually look forward to seeing what

he'll put up there next. The Bramble Board is a conversation piece, something to talk about.

"The tourists will be here soon," I say. Everybody on Cape talks about the tourists.

"Yes," the Poet agrees.

"Actually," I say, "I used to be a tourist, but now that we live here, I'm a wash-ashore. I like the sound of it, don't you? Wash-a—"

"Does your mother have a beau?" the Poet blurts out.

How sweetly old-fashioned, how poetic. A beau.

"I mean a suitor," he mumbles, his cheeks reddening.

Suitor and beau sound like words from *Anne of Green Gables,* one of my favorite books.

"No!" I announce. "She doesn't have a beau."

"Oh." The Poet pauses and looks at me. "You seem happy about that."

"Oh, no, I'm not happy Mother doesn't have a beau. I'm happy that you asked." I realize I'm walking as fast as I'm talking. "Maybe you'll be the suitor to suit her." Oh no, how embarrassing, now I sound like I'm in Green Gables. I sprint three shops ahead.

Then the wind whispers, *Wait, Willa, wait,* and

I muster up my courage, straighten my shoulders, take a deep breath, and turn around. I try to sound nonchalant, like my heart isn't hanging on the clothesline. "Maybe you'd like to come for a picnic on Memorial Day, Mr. Gracemore . . . Sam. Mother was hoping to get to know you better." Then I race off like those tiny piping plover birds when they see giants like me walking toward them on the beach. *Oh, I hope. I hope. I hope.*

CHAPTER 9

Beach Glass

"Hope" is the thing with feathers—
That perches in the soul—
And sings the tune without the words—
And never stops—at all—

—Emily Dickinson

"Nana!" I shout, bursting into Clancy's Candy. "I need your help. I just ran into Sam Gracemore, literally, and I invited him for a picnic on Memorial Day."

"Way to go, Willa," Nana laughs. "Now we're cooking with gas." She hands me a piece of yellow-and-green-striped taffy. "Try this. I'm calling it Lemmego Lime."

"Mmmm, nice, Nana." The smooth candy slides on my tongue and sticks to the roof of my mouth. "Almost as good as Cabot's, but really, what should we do?" I love saying "we." It's nice having a matchmaking accomplice. And Nana's pretty clever for an old bat. That's what Nana calls herself, "pretty clever for an old bat."

"I'm glad you invited him, honey. That ought to get the beach ball rolling."

"But Nana, Stella will be furious. She'll ground me for a week. And the Chatham soccer tournament is next weekend, and if I miss practice . . ."

"Tell Stella I invited him." This would be one of Nana's "little white lies that never hurt a sand flea."

"No, I can't."

"Sure you can. Tell Stella I ran into him in the Stop & Shop in Mashpee and the poor guy's cart was filled with frozen dinners and I felt sorry for him."

"Okay, Nana. I'll try."

Nana ties up a bag of Lemmego Lime. "Good luck, honey."

It's a perfect beach day, and Mother will be at the reception all afternoon. At home I make a tuna fish sandwich and pack a nectarine, chips, soda. I find my sunscreen, pull my towel off the line, then grab a sweatshirt in case it gets windy. Everybody talks about the wind on Cape. *Northeast, south-west, gusty, gale.* We've got as many words for wind as Eskimos have for snow. I throw my stuff in the basket of my bike and sail.

You can get to Sandy Beach down ten different streets, but I always take Bluff because of the words. At the end of Bluff, just before the beach stairs, is an old black chalkboard. Today it says:

Air Temp: 74°
Sea Temp: 59°
Life's a beach, enjoy.

I always wonder who writes the messages. A lonely old fisherman? A retired teacher who still loves the chalk in her hand? Whoever it is, thanks.

At the top of the stairs I rest my bike against a rock and bend down to smell the beach roses, the rugosas. The cinnamon-sweet pink flowers grow wild all over the Cape.

And then there's the sea. There's something amazing about that moment when you first see the water. You may have seen it a thousand times before, but each time is brand new. It makes my heart sing, it's so beautiful. And they say once you fall in love with old Cape Cod, you never get the sand out of your sneakers.

Today the waves roll calmly in and out. A red-striped umbrella flaps gently in the breeze. A curly-haired boy sticks a feather on a castle. A couple walk holding hands. A sailboat glides by. Terns scamper across the sand. One seagull lands and, like a relay, another takes off. *Caw . . . caw . . . caw-caw-caw-caw-caw.* I close my eyes and soak it in. *Thank you.*

I spread my beach towel on the sand and open my lunch. Nectarine juice dribbles down my chin. The tuna fish is perfect. I make it the way Nana does, just plain with mayonnaise. Stella makes it with tarragon, curry, and raisins. Too foo-fooey for me.

After lunch I walk along the water, sun shining on my face, searching for beach glass. Bottles left on the beach or thrown overboard get swept up by waves and smashed against rocks into small pieces. Over time the jagged edges are sanded smooth.

I have an old mayonnaise jar on my windowsill filled with the beach glass I've collected over the years. Mostly greens, whites, and browns, some blues and reds. I call it my rainbow jar because it's very good luck to find a pebble of beach glass amid all the sand and shells and stones onshore. You have to look closely.

Yes. A blue. My favorite. I wash it, dry it, and put it in my pocket. I keep walking to the end of the spit, nearly a mile, find an orange jingle shell, then head back.

Stomach down on my towel, I stretch and curl my toes in the sand, and open *The Member of the Wedding,* by Carson McCullers. This girl Frankie, who's twelve, feels left out. Like she's not a member of anything. Moving as often as we have, I never really felt like I belonged either.

Here in Bramble, though, it's different. I've got Tina and Nana, Mr. Tweed and Sulamina, and if things go well at the picnic, my impossible wish might just come true.

For as long as I can remember, I have wanted a father. Way back in nursery school there was this girl named Mattie Moran, and every day when her father came to pick her up, she'd giggle and run off to hide. Mattie's father would open cabinets and sort through the dress-up box, saying, "Did anybody see my Mattie? Where's Daddy's little girl?"

When he found her, he'd swing her up high in the air and she'd giggle even louder.

Sam Gracemore would be a wonderful father. He's smart, kind, handsome, and funny without even trying. He's got a good job. I don't think there is any more important job in the world than being a teacher. He loves poetry and books, like me. And he made Stella smile. I've never seen Mother smile at a man the way she smiled at Sam that open-house night. I think the Poet has a hole in his heart, just like Stella, and if she'd just give him a chance, they could patch up those holes together.

The girl in the book, Frankie, is jealous that her older brother's getting married. Someday I want to get married. Right now the only wedding I care about is the one that gets me a father. I wonder if Stella would plan another big, fancy wedding?

You should see Mother's work. It's amazing. Even though she tries to keep me away from the weddings, I've been sneaking in to watch for years. When people say how perfect everything is, I want to jump in and say, "That's my mom. My mom did that."

I love every ingredient—the music, the flowers, the food, the dancing. The bride is always glowing.

The groom is always nervous. The bridesmaids giggle. The ushers joke. The flower girls and ring bearers chase each other around.

And then there's the father of the bride.

I can take the look on the father's face when the music starts and he smiles and whispers, "Are you ready?" and his daughter looks up at him and nods like she's trying not to cry, and then he stiffens his arm and winks at her and they start processing. And I can take it when they reach the groom and the father kisses his daughter goodbye, shakes the groom's hand, and pats his back, then goes to sit with his wife. And I can even take it when the father sits up and straightens his shoulders and puts his arm around his wife when the bride and groom exchange vows. I can take all of those things.

But then later, at the reception, when the bandleader calls the bride and her father to the dance floor, and all the relatives and friends grab cameras and circle around to watch, and then it's all hushed, just that father and his little girl in the center of that big ring of love, and the singer starts, "You're the end of the rainbow, my pot of gold. You're Daddy's little girl to have and to hold. . . ." Well, then I have to leave.

A school of fish skip across the water. A sand flea bites my leg. I pull on my sweatshirt. The sun's going down. I take the beach glass out of my pocket and squeeze it in the palm of my hand for luck. I bet the Poet is a good dancer. I bet he likes to walk the beach too. I bet he's great at spotting beach glass. Especially the blues. I bet he'd say, "Here's a nice one, Willa. Put it in your rainbow jar when we get home."

CHAPTER 10

Mirror, Mirror

It would be lovely to sleep in a wild cherry-tree all white with bloom in the moonshine, don't you think?

Lucy Maud Montgomery, *Anne of Green Gables*

"First of all, you must do something with this hair," snivels Ruby Snivler, the unwanted third party at the sleepover at my soon-to-be best friend Tina's house. The three of us are looking at ourselves in Tina's full-length, three-way mirror. Tina and Ruby look like models. Like they're at least sixteen. I stare at my chest and wonder what's wrong with me. Maybe I need growth hormone pills.

"Remember," the Snivler says, as if imparting the wisdom of Solomon, "your hair frames the focal point of beauty: the face."

I wonder which ditzy magazine she got that line from, but I bite my tongue. Tina obviously sees something in this girl. They were best friends before I moved here.

"Here, let me see what I can do," Ruby says, and then yanks my "frame" out of its rubber band. Several brown hairs hang on, screaming, *Help*. Now she's moving my hair up and down like an undecided elevator. "The frame must be perfect. I'd get it cut."

Tina looks up from preparing the manicure bowls. "I like Willa's hair the way it is, Rube." She flips her natural blond hair over her shoulder, end of sentence.

I smile at Tina. "Thanks."

"Whatever." The Snivler shrugs, checking her bleached-blond roots in the mirror.

"Pick one, Willa," Tina says. The display of nail polish bottles loaned by Mrs. Belle for our evening of beauty is absolutely mind-boggling. Just as I reach for a red the Snivler snorts, "Of course, it's nearly summer, girls, so we'll want the melons and peaches. No reds again until after Labor Day, of course."

"Obviously," Tina says. "Everybody knows

that." She dunks my hands into the bowls of bubbly, warm water.

Ruby opens an eye-shadow case, studies the palette of choices, then selects one. She dips her pointer finger into the pot, stretches the canvas, then begins painting. Tina lifts my right hand out of the water, dries it with a towel, then separates my fingers into the pink foam cushion with great finesse. Clearly there is an art to these things.

"How about this one, Willa? That's what I'm choosing." Tina's pointing to an eye-popping hot pink, so bright it begs for sunglasses.

"Perfect," I agree. My best friend and I will have identical nails, if only for one night. Once Stella catches sight of them, they're history.

After Tina's nice mother, Mrs. Belle, delivers the last round of snacks, and after her nice father, Mr. Belle, knocks and pokes his head in, "Hi, girls. G'night, angel," we move on to the moment two of us have been waiting for: the wedding album. The one from the Snivler's aunt Philly Cheeseface's wedding.

"I was the junior bridesmaid, you know."

"Yes, Ruby," I say. "I think the whole town knows."

Tina looks over at me.

"Oh, that's right, of course you do, Willafred," Ruby snaps back like a rubber band. "You are the wedding planner's daughter, after all. And weren't you there, very, very briefly, the day I came for my first fitting? It must be so exciting to have a wedding planner for a mother. Why don't you tell us about some of the most exciting weddings you've helped her with? You know, the glam celebrity ones. Didn't I hear she did K. Jo and Funk Daddy's wedding? Come on, dish us some insider dirt."

"That's not fair, Rube," Tina rushes to the rescue. "That's confidential information. We can't expect Willa to reveal her mother's personal business and . . ."

My eyes are boring holes through the plastic-covered photograph of the Snivler in her lobster-colored junior bridesmaid dress. "Wow, you look so booby, Ruby. Did you get one of those special junior bridesmaid pump-up bras for the occasion?"

Tina coughs. "More cookies?"

The Snivler is snoring, as one would expect. Tina even sleeps pretty. The evening of glamour was wasted on me. Tina is naturally gorgeous. Ruby works hard at it, always trying new hairstyles, studying fashion magazines to be the first girl on Cape with the latest New York trends, but actually she's really pretty too. Maybe I should get more beauty sleep instead of eating cherry cordials and reading all night until my head clunks down on a book.

Tina says Joseph Kennelly likes me, but that's impossible. Tina must be looking in a different mirror. I've got hair that looks like a horse's tail, and a chest that's flat as a book. We haven't even had a conversation outside of school. That would be nice, though. But I'm not losing any beauty sleep over JFK right now. My first mission is to get Mother and the Poet together. Nana says, "Keep on praying, honey, it's not going to be easy. Stella's been wearing those black sunglasses so long it just might take a miracle."

CHAPTER 11

The Labyrinth

As to me I know of nothing else but miracles.
—Walt Whitman, "Miracles"

Walking home from Tina's, I smile at everyone I see. The sleepover was a success. Tina and Ruby are two peas in a pod in some ways, but I can tell Tina sees something in me that's different. Something that she likes.

As I turn our corner the Poet is in his backyard working on the labyrinth. Definition: a complicated network of passages; an intricate or tangled arrangement. You're welcome. I thought I'd save you a trip to the dictionary.

The Gracemore labyrinth is a circle-shaped maze. You enter between two spruce shrubs and walk counterclockwise toward the center. The path is only a few feet wide. You have to walk it alone. The path is bordered by "walls" made out of tall plants and bushes. As you walk you loop in, then away, in, then away, circling closer and closer to the center. It looks confusing, but if you stay on the path, you can't get lost.

When Sam first moved in, Mother hoped he'd "finally get some landscapers in to tackle that jungle of a front yard." But to Stella's great annoyance, Sam doesn't seem to care about the front yard. He spends all his time in the back. Stella watches Sam in the labyrinth from the study window. I can tell she's curious.

The Poet has been adding new perennial flowers all along the labyrinth path. Daffodils, hyacinths, and tulips for the spring. Daisies, brown-eyed Susans, and hydrangeas for summer. Mums and sunflowers for autumn. English lavender and red-berry holly for the winter. Some color for every season. Blue jays, cardinals, goldfinches, chickadees, sing in and out all day. I like the sweet, sad call of the mourning doves—*coo, coo, coo*. There are bird feeders everywhere, and Sam keeps the stone birdbaths filled with water. Sam seems happiest when he's in that garden.

Sam is so handsome. Steely blue eyes, longish

wavy brown hair. Stella just has to fall in love. If you ever met the Poet, though, it's his smile you'd remember. Kind and true. Imagine having someone smile at you like that. Like you were the one thing that made him happiest in the world. We could ride our bikes to school, and on weekends we could work in the garden and talk about books while Stella's busy with the weddings.

I wish I could ask Sam to the father-daughter breakfast in June, but I'm afraid that would spook Stella, so I'm asking Mr. Tweed instead. Tina says some girls are coming with their grandfathers, so that will be okay.

I think Sam would really rather be a writer, but I'm glad he's a teacher. He's the best one I've ever had. I love when he reads poetry to us. Like this English poet, Christina Georgina Rossetti, who lived back in Emily Dickinson's time. I wonder if they knew each other? Anyway, when he read her line "My heart is like a singing bird," I copied it down so I'd remember.

Sam thinks I'm a good writer too. When he read my poem "What Crows Know," which Mother thought was "melodramatic" and Tina said was "sad," Sam scribbled on the bottom of the page,

"Nice, Willa. I like your use of the common crow as a metaphor for perseverance. You've got a way with words." That's the nicest compliment I ever got (and notice he calls me Willa). Sam says, "People are hungry for beautiful words, so if you've got some, plant them around."

Sam's Bramble Board makes Mother furious. Today it reads, BLOOM NOW. I wonder if Sam wrote that? Stella's called Town Hall twice to complain about it "not being appropriate in a residential area." She says, "Next thing you know, some fisherman will tack up a sign and start selling cod on the corner."

Nana says Stella's stretching the taffy, as usual. We think she's afraid of the words, afraid to fall in love with someone who loves them so much. It reminds her of Billy Havisham.

Sorry, I left you in the labyrinth. So when you reach the center of the circle, there's an old stone bench where you can rest awhile. I've watched the Poet sitting there, his face turned upward, eyes closed, smiling. I'm not sure whether he's thinking or praying or what. Anyway, when you are done, you exit walking clockwise, looping in and away, closer and farther, circle after circle, until you end where you began.

"Hey, Willa, hi!" Sam comes out front to meet me. "Beautiful day, isn't it? If you have a minute, I want to show you something."

"Sure." I look up quickly to the window of the study, but I don't see Stella there.

We walk up the stairs of the former Bramblebriar Inn. I bet this place was beautiful years ago. It's still lovely now, like an aging ballerina with that youthful grace.

The Poet opens the screen door. "After you, Willa." The porch is hot and musty. Wicker chairs are stacked in neat rows. I imagine the inn guests sitting on them out under the trees, sipping lemonade. Sam directs me to a table. A long metal container is divided into sections like a giant box of sampler chocolates. There are twenty-six sections, filled with letters, *A*s, *B*s, *C*s—you get the picture.

"Want to give it a try?" Sam asks. He pulls out an old leather album and hands it to me slowly, like it's important to him. It's a journal. The pages are a bit yellowed and frayed from use. I begin to leaf through it, reading quotes from famous writers, some I've seen on the Bramble Board. Some are signed "SG" and dated. Those must be Sam's.

"I've been collecting these for years," the Poet

says. "I knew you'd appreciate it, Willa. Why don't you choose something you like?"

I flip back to the first page. A line from "Miracles" by Walt Whitman.

Sam smiles and nods. "Nice, Willa."

I take out an *A, S, T, O, M, E,* and an *I, K, N, O, W, O, F, N, O, T, H, I, N, G, E, L, S, E,* and a *B, U, T, M, I, R, A, C, L, E, S.*

Together we walk out to the Bramble Board. Sam takes down BLOOM NOW and says, "Go ahead, Willa. It's all yours."

"Thanks, Sam." Carefully I arrange the letters with the proper spaces in between. The Poet and I stand there quiet for a minute. He asks me what he can bring for the picnic, and I say, "Just yourself. Mother is looking forward to getting to know you better." Sam looks at the board and smiles at me as if to say, *Keep your fingers crossed.*

I look up to the study. Was that Mother at the window?

That night I can't stop thinking about the picnic. I hope Stella wears something pretty.

CHAPTER 12

Blue Like the Sea

Better by far you should forget and smile
Than that you should remember and be sad.

—Christina Georgina Rossetti, "Remember"

"Willafred Havisham, how could you!"

Mother is furious about the picnic. Nana had a good idea, but when we were driving home from soccer (we lost 4–2), I decided to tell the truth. Besides, my face gets red when I lie and Stella can always tell.

"You call him right now and say you're sorry. We're going off Cape that day."

"But Mother, that would be a lie. And he'll see us having our happy little picnic when he's out walking on that lonely widower's walk, and he will probably be overcome with a horrible sadness at the thought of spending another holiday without the company of his loving wife and son and then be so overcome with despair that he'll fall down on his knees, sobbing, on the ground. And besides, Mother, you like him. I know you do. He's charming and handsome and has such a nice way with words."

The last part is more than Mother can bear. She sinks down in the white wingback chair and sighs loudly. "Oh, Willafred, you are so melodramatic. I know what you're trying to do. You've tried it before, and I'm warning you, stop right now."

A photo album of faces flips through my mind—Bruce Carlson, Joe Petras, Chuck Jordan, Joe Jewel, Zane Friday, Fred Miller, Wayne Castronovo, Mike Byron, Jerry Jennings, Bill Kahl, Dennis Tompkins, Ned Trombley, Joe Scotti, J. C. Simille. All nice, smart, handsome men Stella dated—potential husbands for her, potential fathers for me—in previous towns, but Stella always got scared.

"I will not, repeat NOT, have my daughter playing *Fiddler on the Roof* with my life. I do not need a matchmaker. I don't want to be matched. Now, go finish your westward-expansion essay, Willafred. I feel a migraine coming on."

Mother raises her hand to covers her eyes, blocking the sight of me.

Me, Mother, me. What about me? "Oh please, Mother, don't be afraid. Take a chance. You're so close this time. Can't you just open up your heart one tiny bit more?"

Mother's chin sinks below Mexico. She comes slowly toward me and looks into my eyes. Father's eyes. *Sparkling like the sea on a sunny summer day.* That's how she described them in one of the poems locked away in the red heart. Mother doesn't speak. She stares into my eyes as if searching for something. Her face softens a bit, her lips tremble, her arms rise as if to hug me. Then, abruptly, she turns away.

"I have no heart left to open, Willafred. It's buried at the bottom of the sea."

Stella heads down to her studio. I listen at the top of the stairs. After she closes the door, I go to her room and get out the heart-shaped trunk. Each time I unlock it, the scent of cherry nearly makes me faint. The trunk is filled with the letters and poems Father and Mother wrote to each other while he was in Europe and she was in Washington planning their wedding. The heart is filled with love.

I hope our children have your blue eyes, Billy,
sparkling like the sea on a sunny summer day.
Love always, Stella

I gently lift another piece of yellowed paper and touch the swoopy lines. I can almost feel the warmth of my father's hand as I trace the words he wrote to Mother.

> *Mere words cannot paint my love for you,*
> *I long for the day when we say "I do."*

I hold the letter against my cheek. It's comforting, like a kiss.

Then there's a funny one from Stella. It seems she once had a sense of humor:

Billy, I'm no poet, but here goes it. . . .
I'm eating the cherries and tossing the pits,
Just hope all this chocolate won't turn into zits.

I always thought it was good that Stella kept these poems. Now I wonder. Like that Rossetti poem. Maybe it's better to forget, if remembering makes you sad.

There's a brown smudge on the corner of another poem. I smile and raise the old paper to my nose, inhaling the memory of the cordials Mother ate the day she first read it. I bring the letter to my ear and it rustles against my hair. *I love you, Willa, I love you.*

Later I do some soccer drills, then bike over to Tina's house. She has a good idea. "Why don't you invite Sulamina Mum and that old guy Mr. Tweed to the picnic too? I don't think they have any family on Cape, and then it will seem more like a party, rather than some private date you've arranged for your mom and Gracemore."

Tina may be long on glamour and short on grammar, but she can sure conjure plans in a pinch. "Thanks, Tina." I head straight for Mum's.

Sulamina Mum is the minister of Bramble United Congregational, "BUC". We're all united, but you can believe what you believe, and I'll believe what I do. Sulamina says, "Call me sister," but everybody calls her Mum. It fits better. When Mum took over BUC, according to Nana, she brought a whole new kind of religion to Bramble, "a little bit of this and a little bit of that." It doesn't matter what religion you come from or whether you subscribe to any formal religion at all, everyone's welcome at BUC. Jews, Catholics, Buddhists, Baptists, we blend like a bouquet. And boy, can we sing. My favorite song is an old Shaker hymn called "Simple Gifts."

Mum says, "If you're searching for meaning, search no longer. The buck stops at BUC. We've got a real simple prayer here. Just two words: *Thank you.*"

Every Sunday morning Mum's crazy-colored robe fills the doorway of that old white building like a rainbow. Her face is the sun in the center. She welcomes and hugs each and every person, young or old, rich or poor, like you are that one special, beloved, long-lost daughter or son who finally found the way back home. If you ever met Mum, it's that hug you'd remember. I think Sulamina Mum is the holiest person I ever met.

Mum's sitting on the steps in the sun. When she sees me, she says, "Hallelujah, here comes the love." I laugh and wave.

When we first moved to Bramble, I thought Mum said that to everybody, but then I realized it was just for me. When I asked what she meant,

Mum whispered so Stella wouldn't hear. "I know when love is working its magic. Your secret's safe with me, little sister."

Mum says, "Thanks for the invitation, Willa. I'll be at that picnic with bells on, and tell Stella I'm bringing a watermelon. We'll have some seed-spitting fun."

After Mum's I head to Bramblebriar Books. Muffles is in the window sleeping in the sun. The store is busier than usual. Already the tourists are coming.

"I'd love to come for a picnic, Willa, and I'd be honored to escort you to the pancake breakfast. Ever since Nora died, I don't get invited to a lot of shindigs. And you said your grandmother is going to be at the picnic?"

Mr. Tweed seems particularly happy about that. I think he likes Nana.

I tell Mr. Tweed that I'd give Jane Austen's *Persuasion* a seven out of ten, kind of heavy for my taste. I like *Emma* better. When we finish our tea, he says, "Muffles is keeping a new book warm for you," and I go to the window ledge to pick up *Little Women,* by Louisa May Alcott.

✻ ✻ ✻

Patient as a tomcat waiting for a mouse, I sit quietly as Mother reads my essay, "Wagons of Hope Heading West." She's pleased, so I pounce, stealthily slipping in Tina's plan as Mother eats dessert.

The wedding planner is rating the cranberry mousse left by an aspiring baker from Harwich who would love to get some of her business. Stella's mind is on Moira Hennessey's wedding. It's just two weeks away, and from what I've gathered eavesdropping through the floorboards, Mother still hasn't convinced Mrs. Hennessey that "McNamara's Band" is not an appropriate substitution for Beethoven's "Ode to Joy."

"So, does that sound okay, Mother?" I ask again.

"I suppose so," she says. "We've got to do something on Memorial Day."

Then, *poof,* the wedding planner is off again. Back to her imaginary conversation with Moira's mother, working through various arguments. Stella will know the winning line when she thinks of it. Stella's the leader of the bridal band.

Later, when I put some folded laundry on Mother's bed, I notice the book of poetry I gave her on her nightstand. Ooh. Yes. Good sign.

CHAPTER 13

I'm eating the cherries and tossing the pits,
Just hope all this chocolate won't turn into zits.

—Stella Havisham

"Joey Kennelly definitely likes you," Tina whispers at lunch, flipping her hair back, exclamation point. "He keeps looking over here."

We spy over toward the seventh-grade boys' table. I may have imagined it, but this morning when I bent over to pick up that pen, I think JFK smiled at me. He's tall and thin with sandy brown hair and blue eyes, sort of quiet or maybe shy, I'm not sure which, and he doesn't make fun of stuff in class like some of the guys do. I take another bite of tuna fish, made Stella's foo-fooey way but I'll deal, and wipe my mouth quickly. I sit up straighter and fix my hair. "Why do you think he likes me?" I whisper to Tina.

School cafeterias in my other towns were so loud you'd have to shout to tell a secret (if you had someone to share a secret with, that is), but at the very respectable Bramble Academy "young ladies and gentlemen" are expected to use "superlative manners at all times, including in the classroom, on the playing fields, and in the dining hall." Mother gets hot flashes just thinking about all of the lovely rules at this place.

"I see him looking at you in class. Hey, maybe he'll ask you to dance at the June Bug. What are we going to wear, anyway?"

The "we" is music to my ears. What are "we" best friends going to wear to the seventh-grade end-of-year June Bug dance?

Speaking of bugs, Ruby Snivler plunks herself down with her two big overgrown ears of corn. "Hey girls, did you buy your tickets yet? The Bug's only four weeks away. I hope Joey Kennelly comes. If he does, I'm getting him to dance. . . ."

Oh great, the Snivler likes JFK too.

"Did you know I'm on the Bug committee? I'm in charge of decorations. My sister, Wanda—you know her, Tina, isn't she beautiful?—is going to help me when she gets home from college next week. Wanda was crowned queen of the Junior Jubilee at Pillowamba U., and she's got lots of glam ideas. And guess what? *She's engaged!*"

Glam grates on me like fingernails on a blackboard. It's one of Tina's favorite words too. For a second I feel sorry for Ruby. It must really hurt to lose your best friend. And it must be annoying to have a mother who wears more makeup than a clown.

Ruby takes a loud slurp of her beefy noodle soup. "And remember, watch those calories. We want to look good in our gowns."

"Gowns?" I echo. "We're supposed to wear gowns to the Bug?"

"Any nice dress will do," Tina says. "It doesn't have to be a gown."

The Snivler rolls her eyes. Clearly Tina has it wrong. "I mean fancy evening attire, of course. I'm having my bridesmaid gown hemmed to cocktail length . . . slingback heels, beaded shawl, Mother's diamond teardrop earrings—they're *real diamonds*. Mom says I have to look sophisticated, since I'm on the Bug committee and . . ."

The Snivler drones on and on. Suddenly I've

lost my appetite. Getting Mother to agree to the Bug is going to be brutal. No way is she going for the gown.

"You're so lucky, Willafred." The Snivler says my name like it's a mosquito bite. "Being a wedding planner's daughter, you can just walk downstairs in your own house and look through the sample racks to find a gown for the Bug. Oh, wait . . ." She pauses for dramatic effect. "That's right. You're not allowed in—"

Before I can think of a zinger, Tina clicks in. "Actually, Rube," she says ever so matter-of-factly, "my mother is taking me and Willa shopping for dresses next Saturday."

JFK is walking slowly toward us. He has to pass right by our table to put his tray on the conveyor belt. Thankfully the Snivler's snout is deep in her bowl, sucking up the last drip of beefy noodle soup, and she doesn't notice him smile at me as he passes our table. *Oh my God, he's got a dimple.*

"See? I told you, Willa!" Tina forgets to whisper.

"Told her what?" The Snivler looks up, soup dripping off her lip.

"Oh, nothing," Tina covers. "We're late for science, that's all."

I sit in chemistry lab staring out the window as my poor lab partner, Rachel Strichoff, tries to simultaneously observe and record the effects of rising temperature on the vial of blue water bubbling over our Bunsen burner.

"What are you smiling about, Willafred?" asks Mrs. Dour, our science teacher.

"Just thinking about how far we've come as chemists this year, Mrs. Dour."

Actually, I'm thinking about how far I've come with my wishing. Bramble feels like home. Tina's just about my best friend. JFK *smiled at me.* No statue faces or suitcases from Stella yet. And the Poet's coming for a picnic. Later he and Stella will take a moonlit walk, fall hopelessly in love, date all summer, get engaged in the fall, and get married in December, and when my lucky thirteenth birthday arrives in January, I'll blow out those candles, open my eyes, and look right at my wish come true. A father.

I rush home to get a head start on homework to put Mother in the best possible picnic mood. Next week Nana and I are really going to have to cook up a good way to broach the Bug with Mother, not to mention the gruesome gown ordeal.

That night I keep reading *Little Women*. Mr. Tweed was right. I love this book. Especially Jo. I start to nod off, then remember Moira Hennessey's wedding. I take a cordial from the box hidden in my bookcase. The chocolate sticks to my hands. I'll have to find a better place now that it's getting so warm. Mmmm. Delicious. I grab the satin satchel and tiptoe downstairs. Moira's dress is lavish with layers of frill. I finger along the hem until I find a good spot. It takes only a minute to sew things up.

CHAPTER 14

The Picnic

For the rest of the week she talked picnic and thought picnic and dreamed picnic.

—Lucy Maud Montgomery, *Anne of Green Gables*

I'm standing in front of the mirror, trying on tops for the picnic. I swear I've gotten two inches taller since we moved here, but I'm still so skinny I need a belt to hold my shorts up. And when will I ever get a chest? I'm dreading the beach this summer. Tina and Ruby will be bopping around in bikinis like in a Victoria's Secret commercial. Not that Stella would ever let me wear a bikini, but if I could, it would be nice to have something to bop.

Mother's on the phone talking to a mother of the bride. "Excuse me?" she asks in that slickity-sweet, New York, so-swift-you-don't-realize-you've-been-sideswiped voice, "a *bobcue*?" Mother looks at me and rolls her eyes. "Huh, huh . . ." She points to the bagels on the counter. That would be breakfast. Stella's not one for leisurely brunchfests. If I want one of those, I head to Nana's. Bacon, eggs, waffles, sausage . . . and a pot of piping-hot tea. That's how Nana and I take our tea. Piping hot, with milk, no sugar.

The wedding planner was up at 5:00 A.M., probably replaying in her mind Moira Hennessey's wedding, which from what I could see through the window, looked like it went well. Mother has had her orange juice, vitamins, black coffee, and organic yogurt. She's devoured the *New York Times* and *Wall Street Journal,* pen and paper in hand to jot down wedding to-dos and stock ideas to discuss with her broker. She has run five miles, has showered and dressed, and is now on her second cup of coffee when most of the Cape, most of the country, is just waking up.

"No, I'm sorry, Mrs. Mobil, we can't possibly do a *barbecue.*" Mother taps her pen impatiently on the table and sighs her signature sigh. "Yes, but this is *Cape Cod,* Mrs. Mobil." Stella says "Cape Cod" like one might say "the White House" or "Buckingham Palace." I spread peanut butter on a bagel and try not to appear like I'm paying attention.

"A clambake on the beach for the rehearsal dinner is a possibility, but I don't do *barbecues* for weddings."

The menu for our picnic is posted on the refrigerator. Grilled teriyaki tuna steaks, roasted red potatoes, asparagus, and assorted greens with blueberry vinaigrette from Panache, a gourmet deli in Cotuit. When Nana heard the menu, she rolled her eyes. "Tell Stella I'm bringing the good stuff. Tuna luna, who wants diet food at a picnic?"

It's a perfect Cape Cod day. Warm and sunny, crystal clear blue sky.

Sulamina Mum arrives first. She's wearing loopy fish-shaped earrings and a pink-and-yellow fish print skirt and is carrying the biggest watermelon I've ever seen. I decided to let Mum break the spitting contest to Stella herself.

Next Nana drives up in her old Volvo station wagon. "Give me a hug, shmug." Her trunk is filled with the fixings for a good old American picnic. Hot dogs, hamburgers, potato salad, deviled eggs, even a red-white-and-blue carousel you twirl for ketchup, mustard, and relish. I can smell

Nana's lavender lotion. She's got a bit of red lip-stick on.

Next comes the Poet, wearing jeans and a white pocket T-shirt. He's carrying a small bouquet of lilies of the valley from his labyrinth. Mum whispers to me, "Mmm—mmmm. Now, that's a fine-looking man."

The Poet's fine looks aren't lost on Stella, either. She blushes when she takes the flowers. "Why, thank you, Sam." She sniffs the tiny white bell-shaped flowers. "Lovely."

"The pleasure's all mine, Stella," the Poet says, smiling that smile that could melt Alaska. He called her Stella. Just like Nana does, just like her friends probably would if Mother ever had time to make any. Mother prefers Estelle or Ms. Havisham with clients. The Poet turns and winks at me, then shakes hands with Nana and Mum.

Mother looks especially pretty today. She's wearing red linen shorts and a white blouse; her black hair is shining in the sun. Neither the Poet nor I can stop looking at her. Who couldn't fall in love with Stella Havisham? She's gorgeous and successful. Glamour sure didn't stand in the way of her greatness. She will be such a beautiful bride.

I can see it now. Maybe we should wait until spring to do the wedding. Then the *Cape Cod Times* can read: "The bride circled toward the groom, waiting in the center of the old Gracemore garden labyrinth, in bloom with fragrant hyacinths, daffodils, tulips, and . . ." No. I want the wedding in December. Then I can have my January birthday wish.

Mr. Tweed arrives last, dressed in checked Bermuda shorts and matching cap, carrying a bottle of wine. He removes his hat, bows, and kisses Mother's hand. "Delighted, I'm sure." Then he kisses Nana's cheek. "Violet." He nods and winks.

Mr. Tweed just winked at my grandmother, called her Violet, and kissed her!

"Violet" turns red and laughs, fixes her collar, touches her hair, and turns to see if Stella noticed. Stella is too busy talking to Sam. But Sulamina Mum and I noticed.

After dinner Mother and Mum bring the dishes into the kitchen. Nana and Mr. Tweed set up the wickets for croquet. Sam asks if I want to kick a soccer ball around.

"I'd like to come to one of your games, Willa, if that's all right."

"Sure, that would be great."

"I played a bit in college," he says.

When it starts to get dark, Mother flicks on the outdoor lights and brings out some citronella candles to keep the bugs away. Nana whips out a bag of marshmallows and asks Sam to start a fire in the old stone fireplace so we can roast them. I bet the lemon mousse with raspberry sauce from Sheer Confection will be good, but Nana's right about the marshmallows. It's not a picnic without marshmallows.

Sam and Stella are talking, and I hear snippets of their conversation. Mother says, "Washington, twelve years ago," and I see Sam reach out to touch her shoulder. Mum starts asking me about school, and the next thing you know, Sam and Stella are gone. I go inside to look for them. Up in the study I look over at Sam's backyard. There they are, in the labyrinth. Actually, they're walking slowly around the outside. Sam is pointing to things and Stella's nodding like she's interested. Stella says something and Sam laughs.

Oh, this is good. Good. Good. Good. Back outside I play a round of croquet with Mum. Then Mum and Nana and Mr. Tweed and I play. Later, when Mother and Sam come back, Mr. Tweed uncorks the wine and pours glasses for the grown-ups. I look for a stick, just the kind Nana taught me, a young one, still green in the middle so it won't catch on fire, and I sit down to roast that first marshmallow of the summer.

Tina stops by and we go out to the front porch so we can talk about the June Bug. Even out there I can hear laughing from the backyard. "It's going great," I say. "They went for a walk by themselves, and Mother seems so happy."

After Tina leaves, I head toward the backyard, but before I get there, I hear a strange, gasping, clucking sound, like someone's choking, and I run.

It's Mother. Giggling. Not laughing, giggling. Head back, chest heaving, hands on her stomach, tears in her eyes, all the teeth showing, letting it rip, roaring out loud, giggling. I realize I must look shocked, but I've never heard Mother giggle before. And the best part is that she's clearly giggling over something the Poet has said.

Yes. Yes. Thank you.

"I'd like to propose a toast," Mr. Tweed says.

I grab a can of root beer, and the grown-ups raise their glasses.

"For every mind there is a reason, for every heart there is a season, and as we herald the arrival of summer, on these shores we so adore, may we be grateful for our blessings and open wide our hearts to love."

Just then the wind picks up and blows out the candles. I rush inside to get some matches, and when I return, Stella has drawn a black sweater on over her pretty white blouse. She looks like she's at a funeral, all traces of giggling gone.

Nana and Mr. Tweed are talking quietly in the corner. Mum is carrying the watermelon inside. No way are we spitting seeds now. The Poet is looking from Mother to me, from Mother to me, as if watching a tennis volley, hoping one of us will explain.

It was that last word Mr. Tweed said that did Mother in.

It was the "love."

Father's Day

> *"I'm so full of happiness, that if Father was only*
> *here, I couldn't hold one drop more," said Beth. . . .*
> *Half an hour after . . . , the drop came. . . .*
> *Mr. March became invisible in the embrace of four*
> *pairs of loving arms.*
>
> —Louisa May Alcott, *Little Women*

Amy, Beth, Jo, and Meg. The four sisters in
Little Women love their mother, Marmee, and their
father so much. When Mr. March comes home
from the war on Christmas Day, it is their best
present ever. Jo's my favorite. She's the writer.

When I was younger and first learned about
how Father died, I remember hoping that someday
he'd show up at our door. It was some other guy
who got tangled in a hot-air balloon and drowned in
the ocean. My father, Billy Havisham, had somehow

parachuted to safety and got amnesia when he hit the ground on a deserted island, and then one day a coconut clonked him on the head and his memory came rushing back, and he remembered Stella waiting in Poet's Park and spent years tracking us all the way up the East Coast until he found us.

I always dread Father's Day, but this year it won't be quite so bad. Mr. Tweed, who if you had to make up a grandfather, would be just the kind you'd imagine, is taking me to the Bramble Academy Father-Daughter Pancake Breakfast.

I put on a green-and-yellow-checked skirt and yellow blouse and tie my hair back in a yellow ribbon. I look like an eight-year-old. I wonder what Tina is wearing.

Mother is on the phone. No seventh day of rest for the wedding planner. This is high season, and after *Cape Cod Life* magazine featured her on the front cover of their last issue, the phone has been ringing off the hook. Mother looks up and nods at me, but she's clearly picturing the person on the other end of the phone.

"Who do they play? Duke and Dora? *D-o-r-a*?" Mother is furiously writing notes. "*Forever Young*? No, I've never seen it, but it sounds vaguely familiar."

My heart is pounding. Duke and Dora. Tina's favorite couple. Her favorite show. Wait till she hears.

"Well, what's the bride's real name? Candi with an *i*. And his? Randy with a *y*. Okay. *This* Labor Day? Impossible! What's the budget? *How much?* Really? Well, maybe we can work something out. Yep, yep, uh-huh. Certainly." Mother looks up at me. I act like I haven't heard a thing. "Absolutely. Not a word. Completely q.t."

Duke and Dora are getting married! In real life! Here on Cape Cod! And Mother's planning their wedding! Tina is going to go nuts.

"Bye, Mother," I say when Mr. Tweed pulls up. Stella gives me the busy *ta-ta* wave. I wish she'd take a picture of us or at least come and say hello.

Mr. Tweed, dressed in a tan suit and yellow bow tie, hands me a bouquet of yellow carnations. They smell so nice. Simple and nice.

"Thank you, Mr. Tweed. Yellow's my favorite color. How's Muffles doing?"

"Oh, fine, Willa. Sitting in the sun when I left. Thank you, again, for inviting me. I've been looking forward to it all week. What's your grandmother up to today?"

Mr. Tweed drives so slowly, eighteen miles per hour to be exact, stopping at every single corner crosswalk, whether there's a pedestrian there or not. I'm dying to step on that gas pedal. I can't wait to tell Tina the news.

The Bramble Academy gym is decorated in sherbet-colored balloons and streamers. The girls are wearing sherbet-colored sundresses. Some fathers have sherbet-colored shirts and ties to match. Lauren McNulty and her father look so happy together. Trish Johnson, Emily Donovan, and Kelsey Davenport giggle as they walk by. I take a deep breath.

"Hey, Willa, come sit with us. I saved you seats." Thankfully, Tina and Mr. Belle have a table for us. Caroline Shamlian and her father are there too.

"Look, Willa." Tina holds out her wrist. "Daddy gave me a new one this morning." The little gold charm says DADDY'S #1 GIRL.

"Tina," I whisper. "I've got BIG NEWS."

"What?" she says. "Did Joey Kennelly call?"

Mr. Tweed and the fathers discuss the weather. Everybody talks about the weather on Cape. Sunny one second, raining the next. Then they start bragging about their golf scores at the New Seabury course.

"You're not going to believe . . . ," I start, then stop. Ruby Snivler and her father are headed toward us. "I can't tell you here. Top secret. Meet me at the beach at four o'clock."

Mr. Sivler seems nice. He shakes hands with the men, nods hello to us girls. He pulls out a chair for Ruby and pushes it in when she's seated. The Snivler stares like she knows Tina and I have a secret. She looks at Mr. Tweed, then me, then Mr. Tweed again, like she's confused. "Oh, I didn't know you two were related," she snivels loudly. Paige Snyder and Carrie Sorrentino turn and look at us from the next table.

My mouth is full of pancakes. Mr. Tweed rises to the occasion. He clears his throat, pats both corners of his mouth with his napkin, lays it gently on his lap, then turns and smiles warmly at the Snivler. "Oh my, yes. Willa and I go way back. We've been kindred spirits for years."

Like in *Green Gables*. I smile a thank-you to Mr. Tweed and he winks. I can't wait to tell Tina the news. I picked the beach because when she hears Duke and Dora are getting married in *real life* here on Cape Cod, and that Mother is planning the wedding, she'll scream so loud that only the roar of the Atlantic Ocean will drown her out.

Oh my God! When? Where? Willa, you've got to get us in!

CHAPTER 16

The June Bug

Will you, won't you, will you, won't you, will you join the dance?"

—Lewis Carroll, *Alice's Adventures in Wonderland*

Lucky for me, the weekend of the major annual wedding showcase in Boston is the same weekend as the June Bug, and no way is Stella taking me to the wedding showcase. She never takes me to bridal conventions.

Tina's mother, Mrs. Belle, "gaudblessherheart," as Nana says, calls Mother as promised and invites me to the Belles' house for the weekend. "We'll do a bit of shopping Friday night, Estelle, maybe take in a movie. And there's a little get-together at the academy Saturday night. We'll drive the girls, of course, and pick them up."

Stella's so grateful to have a place for me to go

for the weekend and so preoccupied with convention plans that she agrees without a laundry list of questions. And it certainly helped that there was no mention of boys or the gruesome gown.

I never did get to go shopping with Tina and her mom. Stella froze up like a snowman after the Memorial Day picnic, and I couldn't muster the courage to ask her about the Bug. But Tina and her mom went shopping as planned, and after finding the perfect watermelon pink dress for Tina, they found a dress for me and put it on hold.

On Friday night, the night before the dance, we have pizza at Fiorello's and then head to the Cape Cod Mall in Falmouth. The place is packed. Busy, noisy, exciting.

Mother and I never go to malls. Actually, we hardly ever go shopping. Stella orders my clothes from catalogs. She says shopping is a "brain drain," like television.

We enter Macy's and head for the juniors department. I'm embarrassed at the thought of having Tina and Mrs. Belle come in the dressing room. Thankfully, they plop down in gold chairs in the sitting area. I find a room, hang up the dress, and lock the door. I kick off my sandals and get undressed, trying not to step on the silver pins on the rug.

There I am. Just me and the mirror. Front view. Side. Back. Still skinny as a string bean. Flat as a floor. When will I ever grow? And I've got to do something with this hair. Maybe I should take the Snivler's advice and get this horse mane cut.

The plastic rustles as I lift it. Oh, how *beautiful*. Immediately I love the dress. It's deep blue, with tiny bits of silver thread shimmering like twinkle lights. It looks like the sea. The fabric is satiny soft. Oh, please let it fit. I slip the dress on over my head, facing away from the mirror. I'm afraid to turn around.

Ooh, pretty. I look pretty. I do. I smile at myself in the mirror.

It's the color. The blue dress brings out my one good feature. It makes my blue eyes sparkle. I sweep my hair up off my face and turn from side to side. Maybe I'll wear it up like this. It makes me look more glam. I raise my chin and practice smiles. *Sure, I'd love to, Joey.* I sway my shoulders like I'm dancing and laugh.

I can just picture JFK's face when he sees me at the June Bug. It will be just like in the movies.

He'll be talking with Jess Farrelly or Luke LeGraw, and then he'll see me and stop talking. He'll start walking toward me, parting the crowd of dancers, staring at me like we're all alone. When he reaches me, he'll smile shyly, with that gorgeous dimple, and say, "Hey, Willa, want to dance?" Then I'll say . . .

"Hello? Willa?" The knocking brings me back. "How's it look?"

"Sorry, Tina, I'll be right there."

When I walk out of the dressing room, Tina and Mrs. Belle break into matching mother-daughter smiles. They nod at each other like, *We did it,* then rush to hug me.

"You look like a princess, Willa," Mrs. Belle says.

"Wait till Joey Kennelly sees you!" Tina flips her hair, end of sentence.

I'm so happy I feel like crying. Then, just for a moment, I wish Mother were here saying, "Great, honey, perfect dress. I know just the shoes." Then, "Okay, now lingerie." And, "Let's get you some makeup." And, "How will you wear your hair? You can borrow my pearls. . . . Now, let's go get something to eat." At the restaurant Mother would smile and say, "You're beautiful, Willa. You have your father's eyes."

The Belles go through a whole roll of film taking pictures of Tina and me before the Bug. Mrs. Belle fixes my hair in a fancy, braided updo twist, secured with a silver clip. She insists I wear a pair of her diamond earrings to match the sparkles in my dress. Then she applies our makeup, nothing elaborate, just some eyeliner, mascara, a bit of blush. She helps stock our evening bags with lipstick, tissues, and gum.

Mr. Belle is dressed in a tuxedo. His lips tremble a bit when he sees Tina coming down the stairs. He smiles in a half-happy, half-sad way. I bet he's imagining the day when Tina will walk down those stairs in a white dress instead of a watermelon one.

"Your carriage awaits, miladies," he says with a dramatic sweep. He holds the car door open and we get in the backseat, giggling. This is the most exciting night of my life.

I waited all night at the Bug. Like a fly on the wall. Waiting and watching. Every time the door opened.

Every time a new song came on. Every time the Snivler buzzed by, "Why aren't you girls dancing?" before sniveling off to flirt with another boy.

But JFK never came. Actually, none of the really cool boys in the seventh grade came. It was probably the Snivler's tacky decorations.

CHAPTER 17

The Good Guys

Before I built a wall I'd ask to know
What I was walling in or walling out.

—Robert Frost, "Mending Wall"

The Poet has changed the Bramble Board again.
Nana says, "It doesn't take a brain surgeon to solve
that one, honey. He's talking about that ice wall
around Stella's heart."

The day after the picnic the Poet called. "You're
welcome, Sam," I heard Mother say. "No, thanks. I
can't . . . no, actually, I'm tied up with weddings all
summer. . . ." Two days later Sam sent a note.
Stella read it quickly, then threw it away.

I'm not giving up, though. I've got the whole
summer to play matchmaker. Mother keeps looking
out at the labyrinth. She wouldn't be watching Sam
if she weren't interested, but I don't say anything.

Stella's a turtle poking out for a look. If she gets spooked, she's back in that shell in a blink.

When Mother found the pictures from the Bug that Mrs. Belle sent me, she was furious. "You are only in seventh grade, Willafred. *Seventh grade.* Someday I suppose you'll have to go to those silly things, but right now you should be focusing on your schoolwork. I have great expectations for you, Willafred. Don't disappoint me."

That night Mother had a map of the northeast states sprawled across the dining-room table. Maps are never a good sign.

"Why don't you write him a letter?" Tina says at lunch.

"Who?"

"Hello, Willa." Tina rolls her eyes. "Joey Kennelly, *duh*. Ask him to meet us at the beach Saturday. Say a bunch of us from school are going, so he doesn't get spooked."

"No. I couldn't. What if he says no?"

"He won't," Tina says, signature blond flip. "Trust me . . . oh wow, look!"

JFK and the Snivler are walking toward us. *What is she doing with him?*

"Hi, girls," the Snivler says, sticking out her chest, smiling that big, shiny, lip-glossed smile, leaning her head coyly toward JFK's shoulder like she owns him. "Just finished Spanish. We're finally done for the summer!"

Why am I taking French?

"I was telling Joey how I'm having my thirteenth birthday party at *mi casa* next Saturday." The Snivler ignores me but winks at Tina like, *Just follow along, okay?* "We'll go swimming at Wakeby Pond, then over to *mi casa* for a barbecue."

Is "mi casa" all she knows? I'm taking Spanish next year.

"And I said maybe Joey could bring some friends and join us."

His name is Joseph, Joseph Frances Kennelly. JFK to me. The Snivler is batting her eyelashes as fast as a hummingbird's wings. Maybe she'll get dizzy and faint.

"Oh, good," chirps Tina, not missing a hummingbird beat, kicking me under the table. "That sounds like fun. Why don't you bring Luke and Jess with you, Joe?" Tina's always thinking. She's in love with Jess Farrelly.

JFK looks like he's having a root canal. "Sure,

okay," he says, then sprints off.

"Isn't he gorgeous?" the Snivler swoons. "I can't wait to get him alone next Saturday. It's my thirteenth birthday, girls. He'll just have to kiss me."

I expect to hear the *Forever Young* theme song pour like sugar from the dining-hall intercom, but it's just the chime for next period.

My last English class of the semester. The Poet, Mr. Gracemore, Sam, someday Dad, hands back our short stories. He's written "Colorful characters, love the language" on mine. After class we walk out together. "Is everything okay with your mother, Willa? I'm afraid I may have said or done something to offend her."

"No, Sam. You're going to have to be patient. That wall may take a while."

After school Tina and I go to her house. Her room is pink from rug to rafters. Rock stars and soap studs smile at us from every wall.

"You need a new bathing suit," Tina says, case closed. "No way are you wearing that mother thing." Tina strips naked, no big deal, and slides into a pink bikini. She looks like a model. What am I going to wear? Ruby will be bopping on the beach too. I still have nothing to bop.

"Here, try this," Tina says, handing me a yellow bikini. My favorite color. "I bought this last year, but the top was too small."

"Thanks." I try not to sound insulted. "I'll try it on at home. I'm late for the study."

Tina shouts out the window, "Get some dirt on Duke and Dora, will ya?"

"How are the weddings going, Mother?" I ask at dinner, hoping she'll slip.

"Fine, just fine. Now, what are we going to do with you this summer? I don't want you wasting all your time on the beach. I'll ask the headmaster if we can get your eighth-grade textbooks early, then you can at least get a jump start on math and science. Lord knows I don't have to worry about you finishing the summer reading list. Knowing you, it'll be finished by the Fourth of July." This does not sound like a compliment.

"Oh, Mother. I'm invited to Ruby Sivler's birthday party on Saturday. We're going swimming at Wakeby Pond and then to her house for dinner." On Cape we call lakes ponds, not to be confused with "the pond," also known as the Atlantic Ocean.

"Oh, good," Mother says. "I've got the Mobil wedding at Ocean Edge this weekend. The bride, Barbie Jo—actually it's Bobby Jo, but Barbie suits her better, her father's a big Houston oil baron—is being such a prima donna. Her diva mother wanted a *bobcue* for the wedding dinner, and now the daughter insists on having the ceremony on the beach even though there's a sixty percent chance of rain, and it turns out Miss Bobcue is deathly afraid of seagulls—no, actually, she's afraid of seagull *poop*—and what can I do to keep the birds off the beach?"

I sit here barely breathing. Mother is actually talking to me about a wedding.

"Obviously I have no control over seagulls," Mother continues. "What am I going to do, hire guards to shoo them away? They live there, for gosh sakes. . . ." Stella stops cold in her tracks, finally realizing what she's doing. "Enough of that silly stuff."

"No, Mother. I'm interested. I think your work is so exciting. I've got an idea. How about using those fake owls people have on the ocean-front houses to keep the gulls away? You could put them on top of the tent poles and maybe dress them up in blue pin-striped tuxedo jackets to match the groomsmen for a little joke."

"How do you know the jackets are blue pin-striped?" Mother asks suspiciously.

I shrug my shoulders. "I don't know. Lucky guess."

"That's it," Mother says. "Enough wedding talk."

"But I think your work is wonderful, Mother. Don't you love what you do? Making all those brides so happy?"

"It's got nothing to do with love, Willa. It's a job. It pays the bills. It's nothing for smart girls like you to get all goo-goo eyed about so they grow up dreaming of Sir Galahad galloping up to carry them off to the castle. I have greater expectations—"

"But Mother. What if Galahad's a good guy? Aren't there any good guys?"

Mother ignores me and opens a small, handwritten envelope that came in today's mail. I think it's so nice when people write the old-fashioned way.

"Well, I'll say one thing for him. He's persistent." Mother sticks the letter in with the bills. "I'll be in the studio," she says.

I fish out the letter. The Poet has invited me and Mother to his house for a picnic on the Fourth of July, then to see the fireworks in Falmouth Harbor. Just the three of us.

CHAPTER 18

Bathing-Suit Season

It isn't low-necked, and it don't sweep enough. . . .
My silk sacque isn't a bit the fashion, and my bonnet
doesn't look like Sallie's. . . . I was dreadfully disap-
pointed in my umbrella. . . . I know I shall feel
ashamed of it. . . .

—Louisa May Alcott, *Little Women*

I'm standing in front of the mirror with Tina's
yellow bathing suit on. I'm almost thirteen and I
need a magnifying glass to see signs of life on this
chest. At least our uniforms leave something to the
imagination. This bathing suit does not.

Why are boobs such a big thing, anyway? It kills
me the way some girls strut around, pushing them
out proud, like they stayed up all night studying
for them. But still, I'd trade these A's for B's or C's
any day. I can't talk to Stella. Maybe Mum can help.

Sulamina Mum's knee-deep in her vegetable garden staking tomatoes. When I tell her my dilemma, she nearly busts a seam laughing, but when she sees I'm serious, well, then she gets serious too. She stands up and wipes her forehead.

"Come on, girl, let's make some lemonade."

I squeeze the lemons. Mum gets the sugar, cold water, and ice. We take our glasses out to a shady spot. Mum takes a long drink, then puts her glass down.

"Willa, honey, look." Mum hoists up her chest like she's holding two huge cantaloupes in the market. "These here aren't nothing but fat." She laughs, so I do too.

"Don't worry, little sister. Yours'll come. Be glad you're slim. Being big's no blessing. When you get to be my age, breasts aren't nothing but a burden. My friend Glendy had hers surgically reduced, four pounds each side, 'cause her back hurt so bad hauling those babies around. And when Millie Mae stops by for coffee, she has to lean hers on the kitchen table just to take the strain off." Again we have a good laugh.

Each time the breeze blows, the wind chimes clink softly. Mum's stories make me feel better. I guess a small chest isn't the end of the world. Although I wouldn't mind somebody donating me a couple of pounds. Two or three ounces, even.

On the way home I stop by a tourist shop but then decide to go to a nicer store to buy Ruby's present. It is her thirteenth birthday, after all. I pick out an ankle bracelet with a red stone in the center. The saleslady says ruby is the birthstone for July. Maybe that's why her parents picked that name. I find a funny card, and when I step outside, there she is.

"Hey, Willa. I'll see you at Wakeby tomorrow. Guess what? I called Joey last night, and he's coming! Wait until he sees my new leopard-skin bikini. My sister, Wanda, helped me find it. I need a more sophisticated look now that I'm a teenager."

She says "teenager" like one might say "celebrity" or "goddess."

It's late when I sneak back upstairs after sewing the thirteenth secret ingredient into Barbie Jo's gown. I hope the tuxedo owls do the trick for her too. I fish out *Charlotte's Web.* It's one of my favorites. I love the whole words-in-the-web thing.

I have trouble falling asleep. I can't stop worrying about Ruby's party, about how I'll look in that bathing suit. Then, around 2:00 A.M., I devise a plan. All I'll need is a box of tissues.

All of the girls get to Wakeby Pond first. I've got my beach towel wrapped around me like a winter coat. I'm forcing myself to be nice to Ruby, even though she's shamelessly bragging about all the presents she got from her parents. We've got money too, but Stella doles it out like Scrooge.

"He's coming, he's coming," Ruby squeaks, and we all turn and look.

JFK, Jess, and Luke are walking toward us, cool as lifeguards, each holding a beach towel around his neck in just the same way, right grip, left grip, like they practiced it. Boys are so lucky. They just show up at the beach with a towel and a Frisbee or ball. Girls are like camels, hauling blankets, sunscreen, hair stuff, snacks. . . .

JFK smiles at me. That dimple was just for me. Suddenly I feel like beauty on the beach. I whip off the towel and stick out my banana yellow boobs. "Let's go!"

Gazellelike, I dash across the dock, sun on my face, wind whipping my hair, JFK's eyes hot on my back. Gracefully I dive, hit the cool water, bubbles gurgling by my ears. I touch the sand, do a flip, then surface like a mermaid, with long, sleek hair.

That's when I see them. The little white clumps of tissue. Floating around my head like water lilies around a frog.

Lobster red, I dive back underneath and surface yards away like a harbor seal. I hear laughter and look quickly, but thankfully I don't see JFK anywhere. Maybe no one realizes. I swim in fast, run up on the beach, and wrap my towel around me, arms crossed over my chest like I'm freezing. I sit on the sand and call Tina over.

"I think I'm coming down with something. Here's my present for Ruby. Just tell her I'm sorry, but I felt sick, okay?"

Tina knows I'm lying, but she won't tell. That's what best friends do.

At home I take a shower and put on my favorite pajamas. I don't feel like reading.

Tina calls me to report. "After dinner we went down to the basement. I played foosball with Jess. We were having a good time until Ruby turned the lights down and said, 'How about spin the bottle?' Well, you never saw three boys run home faster."

CHAPTER 19

Three on the Fourth of July

And right spang in the middle of the web there were the words "Some Pig." The words were woven right into the web. . . . A miracle has happened and a sign has occurred.

—E. B. White, *Charlotte's Web*

Nana has a Fourth of July date with Mr. Tweed. "We're just going out to eat, no big deal," she tells Mother. "We're going to Wimpy's in Osterville for dinner, then over to watch the fireworks in Barnstable Harbor."

Wouldn't that be something if Nana and Mr. Tweed got married? Maybe they could have a double wedding with Stella and Sam.

Mother said she agreed to accept the Poet's

invitation only because "we have to do something for the Fourth of July" and she'd like to "see the inside of that house," but I don't believe her. I think she can't get Sam Gracemore out of her mind.

Dinner at Sam's is a quiet affair, much less festive than the Memorial Day picnic at our house. I guess because it's just the three of us. Sam has set up a table in the backyard near the labyrinth with candles and a simple bouquet of red, white, and blue flowers. Stella smiles when she sees them.

Sam serves us plates of barbecued chicken, pasta salad, and tomatoes with basil.

"This is delicious," Stella says, somewhat surprised.

"Thanks," Sam says. "I like to cook."

After dinner Sam takes us on a tour of the former Bramblebriar Inn. "There are more than thirty rooms," he says. Most haven't been used in years. Ghost sheets cover the furniture, and cobwebs hang like garland from the chandeliers. It's hot and stuffy, and the old place feels sad, yet there's a definite chill of excitement in the air.

"I had no idea this was so grand," Stella says. She's inspecting rooms like a real estate agent, opening closet doors, knocking on walls, flinging open shades to check the view. I can almost hear her brain clicking, typing mental notes. Stella's up to something.

"I really only use the kitchen and den on the first floor and a bedroom and bath on the second," Sam says. He leads us up another tall flight of stairs. I trace my fingernails through the dust on the banister. "Here's my favorite room," he says.

Unlike the rest of the old Bramblebriar Inn, this room looks lived in and loved. It's painted a cheery sunflower yellow, so bright it's making Stella cringe. Tall wooden bookcases along the walls are overflowing, floor to ceiling, with books. Books, books, books. Instinctively I'm drawn to them. I rub my fingers over the spines, breathing in the leathery smell, wishing I had time to read each title.

"And I thought *my* desk was messy," Stella says. She and Sam laugh. The desk is the size of a dining-room table, covered snow white with papers. More papers are stacked around the room, like buildings of assorted heights. There's a quote from Shakespeare on the wall:

My library
Was dukedom large enough.
—The Tempest, 1611

"I've been working on a book," Sam says, a bit embarassed.

"This desk is magnificent," Stella says. "Mahogany."

"It belonged to old Captain Bramble himself," Sam says. "I found some maps and ship logs in the drawers."

"How interesting," Stella says.

I keep my mouth closed so they don't stop talking.

"Come on," the Poet says, "I want to share something with both of you."

Sam directs us into a narrow passageway, and we follow him up a set of creaky wooden steps toward a blue square above. Step by step it gets brighter. We are walking toward the sky. Then Sam steps out onto the widow's walk and reaches to take our hands. The wind whips against my face. The view of Nantucket Sound is breathtaking.

"See the lighthouse? That's Woods Hole," the Poet says proudly, pointing. "There's Falmouth that way. Cotuit over there. And see that stretch of land way out to the right? That's Martha's Vineyard."

Sam has the most peaceful expression on his face. "Isn't it something?"

"Yes," I say, unable to look away from his face. "It's perfect."

"You should renovate this place, Sam," Stella spouts in her official wedding planner business voice. "You could make a fortune here, year-round. How many working fireplaces did I count, nine? Ten? The bigger bedrooms could be converted into suites with hot tubs. You'd draw the autumn and winter weekenders from Manhattan and Boston. Of course, in season you'd be swamped. And with all of this property and the right event planner you could host conferences, weddings . . ."

Stella sputters on and on, but Sam has sailed out to sea. He's a million miles offshore. Then, suddenly, a cloud crosses his face. "My wife, Maggie, would have loved this," he says. "I still remember Robbie splashing in the water when he was a baby. Maggie and I always talked about someday maybe coming here to live. It was our pie-in-the-sky dream. We could never have afforded this on our teachers' salaries." Sam stares out at the water for a long time. Then his face brightens. "My grandmother loved this old house. When I was a little boy, we used to come up here and make up stories about pirates. I still can't believe what a legacy she left me, like a treasure chest washed up onshore. Sometimes life just amazes you with its goodness, doesn't it?"

Mother is looking at the Poet like she is the one who's amazed. Like, *How can he be so grateful, talking about goodness when he lost his wife and son?*

We're standing so close on the balcony that I can see the gulp in Mother's throat. Her lips tremble and she turns away. Sometimes I forget just how much Stella holds in her heart. *Be brave, Mother, be brave.*

The Poet puts his hand on Mother's shoulder. "I know, Stella, I know," he says. "It's something you never get over."

I see a look on Mother's face that I have never seen before. It looks like hope.

"I've got to go to the bathroom," I say, unable to think of any other way to leave the two of them alone. I hurry down the flights of stairs and run outside to the garden. *Thank you. Thank you.*

Later, on the way to the fireworks, we stop for ice cream at Bloomin' Jean's. I get rainbow sherbet, my favorite, and Stella and Sam both order coffee toffee crunch. As we walk out JFK is walking in with his parents and little brother, Brendan.

"Hey, Willa," he says, looking embarrassed that he's with his parents. "Going to the fireworks?"

"Yes," I say. "Looks like a good night for them." *Duh.*

Stella and Sam are talking quietly, and JFK's parents are trying to get little Brendan to "please decide, before we're late."

"Hey, Willa, maybe we could go to a movie or something this summer."

Did I hear him right? "Sure. I like movies." *Oh help, I sound stupid.*

"Great. I'll call you."

"Great," I say, and rush to catch up with Mother and the Poet.

They are walking side by side, talking in quiet voices, like they are the only people in the world. Just like they did at Open House last fall. From the snippets of words I can catch, they are sharing their stories. *Yes.* I think it's a good sign when people start talking about their past. I don't think you bother telling somebody about your past unless you see that person in your future. I wonder how Nana and Mr. Tweed are doing?

The sky is black, not a cloud in sight. A perfect night for fireworks. We find a spot amid the crowd on Falmouth Heights Beach and spread our blanket on the sand. Mother, Sam, and me. The three of us on the Fourth of July. Just like a family. I wonder where JFK is sitting. I wonder when he'll call about the movies.

Sam sighs a deep, contented sigh and leans back. Mother reaches over, squeezes my hand quickly, and winks at me. "Did you make a wish?" Mother whispers. She means on the stars. Wow, what a poetic thing for Stella to say.

All of a sudden it gets quiet. Everyone is searching the sky, listening for that first *boom*. I find the biggest star (it's probably a planet, but whoop-de-do), then I close my eyes and make my wish. This January, I think it's finally going to come true.

Boom. Boom. Ba-boom-boom-boom-boom. I open my eyes. Reds, yellows, blues, swim like watercolors through my tears. I can't remember when I've felt so happy. There are fireworks in my heart.

CHAPTER 20

Tidal Changes

*She had been forced into prudence in her youth,
she learned romance as she grew older—the
natural sequence of an unnatural beginning.*

—Jane Austen, *Persuasion*

"Hot dang, honey, the tide's coming in." Nana is so happy to hear about Stella and Sam and the Fourth of July. I told her about JFK and the movies, too.

"Listen, Willa, let's not spook Stella just when she's finally got something cooking with the Poet. When that boy invites you out, Alexander and I will chaperone. What Stella doesn't know won't hurt her. We've got to take baby steps here."

Alexander? Mr. Tweed's name is Alexander?

"So how are you and *Alexander* doing, anyway?" I tease her, and Nana turns red.

"Never mind about that," she says, looking to see if any customers heard me. There are quite a few tourists in the store, but nobody from Bramble.

If you're a native Caper or wash-ashore who now calls this place home, sometime right about the middle of July you start complaining about the tourists. Nana calls them the "mental rentals." She says they "drive too fast, talk to fast, expect service chop-chop, and let their ragamuffins dig their dirty paws in my fish." Now, don't get me wrong, Nana loves kids. Especially ones with clean hands.

Tourism is big business here and most of the tourists are great. Everybody loves Cape Cod. Especially the beaches. In 1961, President John F. Kennedy, who loved the Cape, named a national park here. Cape Cod National Seashore stretches forty miles from Chatham all the way to P-town (that's what we call Provincetown). The outer beaches have mountain-size sand dunes and awesome waves for bodysurfing.

Summer is gorgeous here and filled with fun stuff to do, but I like the Cape best off-season. The tourists are back on the other side of the Bourne Bridge, and it's just me and the sea. The wind blocks out everything, and all I can hear is my heart.

Good news! Tina's family invited me to Saratoga for two weeks, and Mother is letting me go. Finally that salt air is dissolving Stella's suit of armor. Or maybe the wind has cleared out the fog in her brain. But weather-related or not, there's been a tidal change in Stella since the Fourth of July. All I can say is those fireworks worked.

Stella and Sam are finally dating. They go out almost every day. Sailing, biking, kayaking . . . They go out almost every night to a movie, play, or concert. They're trying all the hot new restaurants and the local favorites. Mum saw them having breakfast at Moonakis, and Tina swears her parents saw them sing a duet on karaoke night at Liam Maguire's. Oh, to have been a fly on that wall!

When we got home last night, after the Wellfleet Wings creamed us in the final soccer match of the year, I showered and went out to join Sam and Stella. We were going to head into town for ice cream. Walking down the stairs, I heard jazz playing, and through the window I could see them dancing on the porch, Mother's head resting on Sam's chest. Oh, this was good, very good. Just then Stella looked up and Sam kissed her.

Today Stella got up early and packed a picnic basket. They're taking the ferry out to Nantucket, a charming, romantic little island. The perfect place to get engaged.

Nana and I finish weighing the fudge, then wrap the last pieces of her new taffy, Summer Here, Summer Not. She thinks it smells like coconut suntan lotion. I think it smells like sweat. After Kristen and Amy, Nana's two favorite workers, come to take over the evening shift, Nana and I head home to her place.

I love staying overnight at Nana's. She keeps a room just for me with fluffy purple curtains and a patchwork quilt she made. There are lavender-filled pillows on the bed. Whenever I smell lavender, it makes me think of Nana.

I turn the water on in the kitchen sink and start scrubbing the clamshells I dug up at low tide. That's another thing we Capers talk about. High tide and low tide. There's a whole scientific explanation about the gravitational pull between the moon and the sun that causes the rising and falling of the height of the ocean twice a day. But hey, who wants a science lesson? High tide washes your sand castles away, but the waves are better for bodysurfing. Low tide you can wade out to sandbars and dig up clams for chowda.

We don't say "clam chowder" on Cape. We say "chowda." Mr. Tweed is coming for dinner tonight, and chowda is his favorite dish.

Nana turns on some music. She sings "My Funny Valentine" as she sets the table. She's wearing a pretty celery-colored blouse. She has lipstick on. I've never seen Nana look younger or happier. I think Nana and Mr. Tweed are falling in love. I didn't get the scoop on their Fourth of July date, but I know they meet for lunch in the park across from their stores. Once, Tina and I saw them holding hands.

"I think you were right, Nana." I start peeling the potatoes. "That salty air has been wearing away Stella's suit of steel. The Fourth of July was the best."

"Good thing you're going off with Tina for a few weeks," Nana says. "That will give those two lovebirds some time alone. While you're betting on those ponies in Saratoga, I'll be betting on Stella and Sam."

Nana turns on the speckled kettle to steam the clams. I separate the strips of bacon on the griddle with a fork, and the fat sputters. Mmmm, smells so good. Jars of seasonings, Nana's secret ingredients, are waiting on the counter. In addition to the wind, weather, tourists, and tides, another thing Capers talk about is chowda. Everybody's got their own special way of making it. I like Nana's best of all. She's stingy with her recipe, but after all these years I know it by heart.

After dinner I bike to the beach to watch the sunset. There's something magical about the moment when you see that first tiny wink of light on the horizon at dawn or that last bit of orange slip away for the night. There is something so hopeful about it. Someday I want to write about this place. When I have the right words.

I kneel down and write "Some Day" in the sand. I remember Sam talking about *Charlotte's Web* in class one day. How Charlotte the spider wrote "Some Pig" and helped her friend Wilbur. Sam said, "Sometimes a few quiet words strung together just right can change a person's life." Or, in Wilbur's case, a pig's life.

CHAPTER 21

Just a Movie

Whatever you do, don't think I'm in love with Peter—not a bit of it!

—Anne Frank: The Diary of a Young Girl

"You've got to wear something fun," Tina says, flipping through the racks like a professional. Mrs. Belle dropped us off at Mashpee Commons, and we're looking for an outfit for me to wear when we go to the movies with JFK and Jess on Saturday. Well actually, Tina's looking. I have no idea what to look for.

Tina's already got her complete ensemble laid out on her bed. She's had it there since Jess Farrelly called her. The four of us are going together.

"Oh, how nice, a double date," Mrs. Belle said.

"It's just a movie," Tina said, and winked at me.

I thought of telling Stella, especially since she's

been so happy lately and hasn't mentioned the rules in weeks, but Tina said, "Don't risk it."

Nana agreed. "I know the Kennellys from way back. They're a good old Irish family. I'm sure Joe's a fine boy. Stick with the plan, honey. We won't get in your way. Alexander and I will chaperone from afar."

The movie is at four o'clock, and then we're going to Zoe's for pizza after.

Tina picks a short tan skirt and a sea blue scoop-necked blouse. "Here," she says. "Joey never got to see you in your gorgeous June Bug gown. This is almost the same color." Tina comes in the dressing room with me. We both agree, it's a keeper. After, we head back to Tina's to try on sandals and jewelry. Tina tries to help with my hair.

When I get home, Stella and Sam are sitting on the front porch. She pours me some iced tea. "How about a game of croquet?" Mother asks.

"Sure, great," I say. We play until the lightning bugs come out.

After Sam leaves that night, Mother knocks on the door of my room. I'm trying on my new outfit and don't have time to change. "Come in."

"You look nice," she says.

"Thanks, Mother. Mrs. Belle took Tina and me

shopping today. To get some new things for Saratoga. I hope that was okay."

Stella looks at me like she feels sorry about something. "Sure. That's fine." She sits down on my bed, taps her hand on my stack of books, picks up the koala bear I've had since I was little, sets it back down again, and looks around my room.

I can't remember the last time she did that. Just sat on my bed like that.

I sit down next to her.

"You're going to be thirteen soon," she says.

"Yep."

We sit there not saying anything. I can almost feel Stella wanting to keep the conversation going. This is painful for her. I decide to take a leap.

"Mother, now that we're going into eighth grade, lots of the kids at the Academy are starting to go places together, like to the movies, you know, as a group. Not dates or anything. Just a movie and pizza."

"When?" Mother asks. Like she already knows there's a plan. Yikes.

"This Saturday. The four o'clock matinee. Then Zoe's for pizza. Tina's going and Jess Farrelly and Joseph Kennelly . . . and Nana and Mr. Tweed."

Mother rolls her eyes and laughs. "Why is Nana going?"

"Well, she thought if you found out . . ."

"It's okay, you can go. It is the summer and you're almost thirteen. I think we can bend the rules a bit. You worked hard in school all year, Willafred, and I'm proud of you. I have a wedding, but as long as you walk; I don't want you in any-one's car, and you're home by ten, you can go."

Ohh. I feel like crying, like I want to hug her, but I don't want to make too big a deal out of this in case she changes her mind, so I just say, "Thanks, Mother."

"That's a pretty blouse," Stella says, standing up to leave. "It matches your eyes."

On Saturday afternoon JFK and Jess pick me up at Clancy's. Nana stuffs thick bags of candy into our hands. "They'll charge you a fortune at the cine-plex. Have fun!"

Next we pick up Tina, and I nearly die of embarrassment when Mrs. Belle takes our picture. Like we're going to a prom or something. Mr. Belle says, "Got enough money, honey?" and sticks a twenty in Tina's hand.

At the theater the boys buy the tickets, and since I supplied the candy, Tina says, "The popcorn and soda's on me." We finish the popcorn before the previews. When the lights go down, I take a deep breath. It's not a date, it's just a movie.

It's a comedy, and we're all laughing, having a great time. But then the girl finds out her father isn't dead after all. He's the duke of a tiny European country and the girl is actually a princess, and now that he's finally found her, they'll all live happily ever after. "Oh, Daddy. I knew you'd come back for me," the girl says, and he lifts her up and twirls her around the room. A cry catches in my throat and makes too loud of a sound.

JFK pats my hand and whispers, "You okay, Willa?"

"Sure, sorry, I'm fine."

He keeps holding my hand.

After the movie we walk to Zoe's and then to Bloomin' Jean's for ice cream. I've never seen so many stars in the sky.

That night I make the first entry in a journal I bought in town. After seeing Sam's album, I decided I wanted one too. No way am I telling you what I wrote, so forget it. These words are just for me.

Someday I'll look back and read who I was at almost thirteen.

Have you ever read the diary of Anne Frank? When she was only thirteen, Anne's family and some other Jews had to hide away from the Nazis in a cramped warehouse room. Eventually Hitler's men found them. Anne died in a concentration camp just before her sixteenth birthday. But Anne lives on through her words. When I read her diary, I keep thinking she was a teenager just like me. Fighting with her mother, worried about her looks. I'll tell you one thing Anne was lucky about. She got to spend all that time alone with the boy she liked. I'd love it if JFK and I . . .

Mother knocks on my door and I jump. "Yes?"

She opens it and smiles. "What an owl you are. Don't stay up all night, okay?"

Stella is softening, all right. I might actually miss her while I'm away. And I'll definitely miss spying on her plans for Duke and Dora's top secret Labor Day weekend wedding. But I'm excited to go to Saratoga with Tina. I can't wait to get a "Kids' Pix" sheet and watch the horses race and see the ballerinas sipping lemonade.

CHAPTER 22

Summer Vacation

When you do dance, I wish you
A wave o' the sea, that you might ever do
Nothing but that.

—William Shakespeare, *The Winter's Tale*

Isn't that beautiful? Sam read it in class once, and now it's in my journal. Sam said, "No one loved language like old Will. Four centuries later we're still quoting him." And when we crossed the bridge back home today from Saratoga, I swear the wind waved. *Hurry, Willa, you're late for the dance.* Let me tell you, a whole lot can happen when you're away on vacation.

Nana said, "The Princess and the Poet are smitten for sure, and I'm not stretching the taffy." She says Bramble's buzzing about Stella and Sam. "Everyone's wondering when the wedding planner is going to start planning her own."

But that's not even the biggest news. Nana and Mr. Tweed are engaged!

"We were having a picnic dinner on Sandy Beach," Nana said. "Muffles and Scamp were playing. I swear that cat is daft. She doesn't seem to realize Scamp's a dog. Anyway, I turned to get the oatmeal cookies, and when I turned back, there was Alexander with a velvet box in his hand and tears in his eyes. At first I thought, *No, I'm too old for this stuff.* Your grandfather was the love of my life, and we had a long and happy life together. But then Alexander said, let me try to remember his exact words, he said, 'Walk with me, Violet, each day by the sea. My heart is yours. Will you marry me?'"

Is Mr. Tweed a poet or what? And now he's officially going to be my grandfather! But I won't need him to escort me to the pancake breakfast next year. I just know Sam will be my father by then.

And on top of all of that—Duke and Dora's wedding is tomorrow! Tina's so excited I'm afraid she'll have a heart attack. It is going to be spectacular.

The night I got home from Saratoga, I sneaked into the studio. The easels were set with the

Twelve Perfect Ingredients. Dora's (Candi's) gown is "white Duchess of York silk with Swarovski crystals adorning the heart-shaped neckline." The couple will "exchange vows as the sun slips into Nantucket Sound, forming a breathtaking red velvet backdrop."

Gold-and-white-striped tents have been set up on the beach for the reception. Mother ordered cranes to remove seaweed a hundred feet out into the ocean so that none will drift ashore on the freshly raked sand. Tuxedo-clad plastic owls (Stella is still using my good idea) have been stationed to keep the gulls away. And in case it's cloudy, although all weather reports predict otherwise, Stella has ordered thousands of twinkling white fairy lights strung from one end of the beach to the other, so that whether it's cloudy or not, the bride and groom will indeed "dance beneath the stars." Sentries will be posted around the entire perimeter to keep spectators away. Not that any are expected.

From a tall white clipper ship anchored just off-shore the Boston Symphony Orchestra will perform during the dinner of fresh lobster tails and filet mignon. Later, Red Mile Blind (Tina says

Scotto, the hunky drummer, is one of Duke's best friends) will take the stage. The grand finale will be a fireworks show over Nantucket Sound, complete with CANDI AND RANDY, TOGETHER FOREVER written like a rainbow across the sky.

And somehow—only Stella could do it—somehow the wedding planner has managed to keep this the best-kept secret Cape Cod has never known about. Her employees are sworn to secrecy on pain of losing their jobs. The caterers will be quiet or they'll never get any of Stella's wedding business again. Duke and Dora have insisted on privacy, and the wedding planner will not disappoint them.

"So how are we going to get in?" Tina asks. We're enjoying one long, last beach day before the start of school. We walked all the way to the Popponesset Inn and back.

"We'll be dressed up like we're relatives who belong there," I say. "We just have to stay out of Stella's sight. If anyone asks, I'll just say I'm the wedding planner's daughter and you're my friend, and we're assisting Ms. Havisham. Who's going to throw us out? I'm the wedding planner's daughter.

We'll just need to steer clear of Stella."

"This is so exciting," Tina squeals. "I've got to get their autographs."

"No, Tina! Then they'll know we don't belong there."

"Okay, Willa. No problem. Your secret's safe with me."

Just as we're leaving the beach Joseph Kennelly shows up.

"See you later, Willa," Tina says. "I've got to run." She gives me a thumbs-up signal behind JFK's back as she leaves.

"Hey, Willa."

"Hi, Joseph." My stomach is doing somersaults. "How was your summer?"

"Great. My dad let me caddy at Willowbend, made some good money, lots of baseball, soccer camp, windsurfing. Caught a thirty-pound sea bass. How about you?"

"Tina and I went to Saratoga Race Course in New York with her parents. The horses were beautiful. We went to the paddock area and heard the trainers talk to them before the races. Mr. Belle taught us how to bet on the horses to win, place, or show. I picked a couple winners."

JFK smiles—*Oh my God, that dimple*—and says, "Want to walk awhile?"

The waves in the water are no match for the tidal waves in my stomach. We head out toward Popponesset Spit. *Just keep breathing, Willa, and don't say anything stupid.* JFK's feet look so big next to mine. He's gotten taller over the summer. His eyes look bluer now that his face is tanned. I guess mine look bluer, then, too.

It's after four o'clock and the tide is coming in. I move in to avoid a wave and my arm brushes against his arm. Goose bumps. I look at the sand, the water, anywhere but at him.

JFK takes my hand, no big deal, and we keep walking. It feels weird at first, but then I match my stride to his and the holding-hands-while-walking thing is easy.

We talk about school. We talk about soccer. We talk about the boats going by. JFK picks up a piece of driftwood. I pick up an orange jingle shell. After a while we stop talking but keep on walking. Maybe we've run out of topics. *Come on, Willa, think.*

As we reach the end of the spit the wind picks up and a flock of gulls *caw-caw-caw* off noisily, upset we've disturbed them. We stop and look around. It's so peaceful here. No people. Just sky, water, and sand. He asks if I want to sit down.

"I was worried about you at the movies that night, Willa. It must be hard not having a father. My mother told me how he died. That's awful."

"I'm okay," I say.

Then all of a sudden Joseph kisses my cheek. "I gotta get back now," he says.

"Yeah, me too."

The wind subsides as we complete the turn and head back on the calmer bay side. We walk faster, not holding hands anymore. A motorboat full of teenagers zips by, and a girl in a red bathing suit laughs loudly.

"Tell me about your mother's business. It must be cool planning weddings."

"Oh, yes, it's very exciting," I start babbling, grateful to be talking again. "I love helping her. In fact, you know the show *Forever Young*? Well, Duke and Dora, Candi Star and Randy Love in real life, are getting married here on Cape tomorrow, and Mother and I are doing the wedding—"

"Wow! Really? That's awesome."

Oh no, what have I done? "But listen, Joseph,

it's a huge secret, they don't want throngs of fans and TV cameras, so you can't tell *anyone*. . . ."

I stop by Mum's on the way home. When she sees me, her whole face lights up like she's been waiting all day for the sun to shine and finally it just did.

"There's my girl, welcome home. Big news while you were gone, huh? Your grandma and Alexander! I'm so happy for them. And your mom and Sam! Ooh, ooh. They came to BUC last Sunday. See, Willa, it's all good. Love's working its magic."

There's a new line on the Bramble Board:

Unless you love someone, nothing else makes any sense.
      —*e. e. cummings*

Mother and Sam are laughing on our front porch. "Want to join us for dinner?" Sam asks. "We're going to the Impudent Oyster in Chatham."

"No thanks, I'm tired. I'll just make a sandwich." I run to write everything in my journal, then I lie on my bed replaying our walk on the beach over and over again.

Late that night I grab my flashlight and head to the studio to add the thirteenth secret ingredient to Dora's gorgeous gown. I'm nervous. This is such an important wedding. It's hot and my hands are sticky. I hear a noise upstairs and rush to finish sewing. I'm adding extra secret ingredients, since I've heard celebrity weddings don't last long. Duke and Dora might need some extra luck. It's not my best sewing effort, but whoop-de-do, who cares? No one's going to be examining the hem.

CHAPTER 23

The Secret Ingredient

In the garden! But the door is locked and the key is buried deep.

—Frances Hodgson Burnett, *The Secret Garden*

"Willafred, don't forget you're staying at Nana's tonight," Mother says. "I've got a wedding. I'll be late."

It's Duke and Dora's wedding day. Kickoff 6 P.M. September on Cape still feels like summer. It's been sunny and gorgeous all afternoon. Mother won't need those twinkle lights. The sky's so clear there'll be plenty of real stars tonight.

"Oh? Whose wedding?" I ask nonchalantly. We've come so far this summer, maybe she's ready to break Rule #7 and let me near one of her weddings.

Mother stops scribbling notes and looks at me.

She circles closer, then circles away. "Two actors from the city. No one you've ever heard of."

I look out the window at Sam's labyrinth. The garden is in full bloom. He's filling a birdbath with water. I decide to take another leap. A really big leap. "Mother, I know. Duke and Dora are famous. *Forever Young* is the hottest soap." My ears are ringing. I can hear Nana yelling, *Willa, have you lost your marbles!*

"I overheard your conversation months ago. Duke and Dora are Tina's very favorite actors." I charge on, full steam ahead, about how Tina and I are both dying to get into the reception and couldn't we wear our nice dresses from the June Bug and sort of help her out for the day, you know, like wedding planner apprentices?

The word *apprentice* is too much for Stella to bear. Her body stiffens and she says in an icicle voice, "Absolutely not, Willafred." She turns to walk away.

"Oh, Mother, please. Just this time?"

"No, Willafred. You know the rules. I don't want you involved in my business at all. First it will be this wedding, and then the next and the next, and then you'll be daydreaming in geometry and sleeping through science and flipping through ditzy glamour magazines and gushing over soap stars and throwing your whole life away waiting for some knight in shining armor to . . . no, no, no. That's not the life I want for you, Willafred. I have great expectations for you."

"Yes, Mother, so do I. But why does one life have to rule out the other? Can't you be smart and glamorous, too? *You* are. Why don't you want me to be like you? Please, Mother, Tina's my *best friend.* She'll be so disappointed—"

"Oh no, Willafred. Please tell me Tina hasn't told anyone! It's supposed to be a completely private affair. I've been so careful to keep everything a secret. . . ."

"Tina hasn't told a soul, Mother. I'm sure of it. She promised me."

Stella sighs and checks her watch. "Quick, get your stuff together, Willafred. I'm dropping you off at Nana's now. I have a million things to do."

"But—"

"No, Willafred. We're done talking. And if I find that you've disobeyed me and come within two miles of this wedding, you'll be grounded until Christmas."

I'm angry at Mother, but even angrier at myself for crying. I decide to go for broke. "I wish I hadn't added the secret ingredient for you last night," I shout. "I'm the secret to your success, you know."

"What secret ingredient?" she asks in a tired voice. "What are you talking about?"

Finally it's all about to come out. Now she will appreciate me.

But then I see that Mother's not really expecting an answer. She's gathering up her paperwork. I'm already off her radar screen. She's no longer my mother, she's Ms. Havisham, the wedding planner, and it doesn't matter that I'm her daughter.

Nana's working on a new saltwater taffy flavor when I storm in crying. When she hears what happened, she bangs her fist on the counter. Some customers look over. Nana lowers her voice. "Stella needs a swift kick in the pants. Rules, fools. You are going to that wedding, Willa. I'll drive you myself. And that's that."

"No, Nana, please. It will just make her angrier, and besides, things are going so well with the Poet and—"

"Binoculars," Nana interrupts.

"What?"

"Binoculars. You and Tina take a blanket and some binoculars and set yourselves up with a little picnic dinner on the dunes, and you can watch the whole darn thing. Wait, I'll whip you up a basket." Nana heads into the back kitchen and returns in a flash with sandwiches, soda, chips, and a box of Clancy's taffy.

"Tell me what you think of this one, Willa. It's called Brambleberry."

I open the pink wrapper and pop the taffy in. "Mmmm, this is a keeper, Nana. You're going to win for sure."

CHAPTER 24

Duke and Dora's Wedding

I don't ever expect to be a bride myself. . . . But I do hope that some day I shall have a white dress. . . . I just love pretty clothes.

—Lucy Maud Montgomery, *Anne of Green Gables*

"I can't believe you, Willa!" Tina is furious with me for telling Mother about the wedding apprentice thing. Poor Tina is all decked out in her watermelon June Bug dress. She even has matching watermelon shoes and a watermelon purse this time. Her hair's curled up fancy, and she's wearing lots of watermelon-colored lipstick.

I tell Tina about Nana's plan, and since nothing is going to keep her from seeing this wedding, Tina agrees to forgo fashion. We disguise ourselves with fishing hats and sunglasses. Tina gets the binoculars we used to watch the horses at Saratoga Race Course.

"Take the bug spray," Mrs. Belle says. "Those sand fleas can be wicked at night."

Finally we're off. But just as we get to the end of the street Ruby Snivler turns the corner. She's wearing the ankle bracelet I gave her for her birthday.

"Hey, girls," Ruby says, looking us up and down. Tina and I simultaneously take off the fishing hats. "Where are you headed?"

"Gull Beach to watch the sunset." Tina is terrific under pressure.

"But that's a half hour away." The Snivler smells a fish. "You'll miss it."

"Willa's grandmother's driving. See you in school, Rube." We speed off like bank bandits. I turn back to look, but Ruby's gone. What if she follows us?

"Hurry, Willa," Tina shouts. "I want to see them kiss when they say 'I do.'"

When we get near the beach, the first thing I see are the trucks. NBC, ABC, CBS, CNN, *Entertainment Tonight*. Oh no! How did they find out? I turn to Tina.

"It wasn't me, Willa. I swear. I didn't tell anyone."

"Are you sure? Not your mom or dad or—"

"No. Nobody."

"But Tina, you're the only one I told. . . ."

"Maybe Ruby found out somehow," Tina says. "Maybe she overheard us talking."

"Oh, Tina, Mother is going to kill me!"

We park our bikes and race up a dune, scattering sand everywhere. At the top we stop and look down. There are hundreds of people on the beach, all dressed in fancy evening clothes. The gold-and-white tents are billowing in the breeze. The sun is just about to set. Ms. Havisham has outdone herself. I adjust my binoculars and start searching for Stella. "Tina, look, there's Duke, in the black tuxedo."

"Oh my God, oh my God," Tina shrieks, jumping up and down, nearly sliding down the dune. "Isn't he gorgeous?"

I keep searching, then finally I see Mother. She does not look happy. She's barking at a slew of photographers, probably from every major magazine in the country. I feel sorry for her. She worked so hard to keep it a secret. Tina keeps trying to locate Dora, but I keep my focus on Stella. She checks her clipboard and gives directions to several of her staff members. They hurry off to follow her orders.

Then all of a sudden it's quiet. The orchestra begins.

"There's Dora!" Tina screams.

The crystals on Dora's gown glisten all the way up here. With bulbs flashing and television cameras rolling, Dora processes toward her Duke.

"Oh my God," Tina says, "it's like watching them on television, except this is way better than their first wedding."

The air is warm, the wind is light, the waves roll gently against the jetty. The smiling faces of the guests are glowing in the candlelight. Flower girls strew petals along the path. The bridesmaids, in shimmering gold, each carry one long-stemmed white rose.

When the jubilant bride appears in the archway, the flash of camera lights is blinding. All eyes are on Candi as she processes toward Randy, waiting like royalty at the water's edge before the brilliant sunset.

This is Ms. Havisham's finest masterpiece.

"It's absolutely perfect," Tina says. "Your mother

is going to be world famous after this wedding."

All eyes are on Dora. She smiles at Duke. He smiles at her. She is halfway there. But then the smile abruptly leaves Dora's face. She stops and raises the heel of her white wedding shoe to scratch her left ankle. She processes a bit farther and stops to scratch again. That's odd.

Finally Dora arrives and takes Duke's hand. The minister begins. Everything seems fine until Dora reaches down and scratches her ankle again. She says something to Duke. Moments later Dora scratches again.

"What is she doing?" Tina complains. "That's not very glamorous."

Now Duke leans forward and says something to the minister. The ceremony goes quickly. The bride and groom kiss. "Oooooh," Tina swoons. A swell of cheering goes up from the crowd and rises up here to the dunes. Then, to the orchestral rendition of the *Forever Young* theme song, the happy couple process toward the reception tent, smiling and nodding as their guests wave sparklers supplied by the wedding planner.

Then all of a sudden Candi (Dora) Star Love screams like someone in a horror movie. She drops down on the sand, pulls up the bottom of her gown, and starts scratching her legs like a dog. It's hard to be sure, but it looks like she's tearing apart the hem of her dress. She's slapping her ankles, her calves, her knees. Sobbing.

"Oh my God, what's wrong!" Tina is nearly in tears herself.

Duke looks angry. He's calling for someone. The guests are crowding in. The bride is hysterical now. She's shouting something. I search the beach with my binoculars, frantically looking for Stella. There she is. She's slapping a reporter! Oh no. This is awful. *What is going on?*

CHAPTER 25

The Red Trunks

In the little world in which children have their existence, . . . there is nothing so finely perceived and so finely felt, as injustice.

—Charles Dickens, *Great Expectations*

"Willafred, what would possess you to do such a thing? Are you crazy?" It's the afternoon after Duke and Dora's wedding, and Stella hasn't stopped raging.

I try to speak calmly. "I've been doing this for years, Mother. For all of your brides. It's the thirteenth secret ingredient."

Mother screeches like a seagull trapped in a fishing net. She's flapping around the room, shaking her head, slapping a map against the table, looking like she's having a nervous breakdown. Nana would say, "Stella's ready for the funny farm."

"You've been sewing *cherry pits* into the gowns of my brides?" Stella screams, her eyes wide as saucers. "How ridiculous! What on earth for?"

"Mother, your weddings were perfect, but you were sewing your sadness into them, like a spell. I know you didn't realize it, or do it on purpose, but the day after the wedding your brides would start crying and—"

"WHAT? Are you crazy!" Stella's face is red with anger. "Don't say another word." She storms off to her bedroom and slams the door shut.

I guess I should explain. It seems the sand fleas had a feast with the cherry cordial pits I sewed into the hem of Dora's wedding dress, and then they couldn't resist biting the poor bride as well. Finally Dora couldn't take it any longer, and she flopped down on the beach, burst into tears, mascara streaming down her face, and screamed, *"Where's the wedding planner?!"*

Of course, then every reporter in the country wanted that question answered too. Who had ruined the wedding of America's favorite soap-star sweethearts? "Havisham? Would you spell that, please?"

Pictures of Dora scratching on the sand like a

cat with fleas were plastered all over the front pages of the morning papers. It will hit the tabloids and magazines next. Television stations are having a field day with the story. They keep replaying the scene over and over again, with the *Forever Young* theme song in the background. It was the lead story on *Entertainment Now.*

I knock gently on Mother's door and open it. She is lying on her bed sobbing.

"This is an utter disaster, Willafred. My business is ruined. I'll be the laughingstock of Cape Cod. I bet the whole story spread up the arm to Chatham, out and around P-town, down through Truro, Wellfleet, Eastham, Brewster, Dennis, Yarmouth, and Barnstable, and across the Bourne to Boston before the sun rose this morning. People here have memories the size of Moby Dick. I cannot take being the subject of their endless small-town gossiping. I will not be the village fool. We're leaving as soon as I can make arrangements to put this house on the market. I'm done with wedding planning. Once we get settled again, I'm going into accounting or—"

"No, Mother, *please.*" I go in and sit on her bed. My heart is pounding so hard I'm afraid it will explode. "We can't leave Bramble. It's our home. Everything's going so well and—"

"*I'm being sued, Willafred.* Mrs. Love claims I caused her irreparable professional damage and lifelong emotional suffering. I just hope I'm not completely ruined financially. This is a disaster. How could you be so foolish? Cherry pits in wedding gowns! That's just the sort of dreamy-eyed, nincompoopish fairy-tale drivel I was afraid of. I wanted more for you, Willafred. It was a mistake to come here. Nana's obviously encouraging this behavior. Then we've got the guy next door hanging poems on his front lawn and walking in circles in the back. . . ."

"He's not 'the guy next door'! He's Sam. He loves you, Mother. You love him."

"*Love?* What can you possibly know about love, Willafred?"

"But I thought you were getting married."

"*Married?*" Stella stands up. "Married? I have no intention of . . ."

And then there it is. The statue look I've been dreading. Stella's turning to stone before my eyes. There's the armor, the helmet, the shield. . . .

I turn and run, slamming the door behind me,

down the stairs, past the wedding planner's studio, out of the house, and down the street. I can't go to Tina's. I'm still mad at her for giving the secret away. If all those reporters hadn't been there, this wouldn't be such a disaster. I run to Nana's. She's not home. I head toward BUC.

Sulamina Mum is sitting on the front steps throwing bread to the birds, like she's been waiting for me, like she knew for sure I was coming.

"Have a seat, little sister," she says, patting the spot beside her. Mum takes my face in her hands, looks in my eyes, and smiles. "Mmmm-mmm-mmm, if that isn't the prettiest blue in the world. You make the ocean jealous." I lean my cheek into the palm of Mum's hand. Without a word she puts her pillowy arms around me and lets me cry.

I remember the first time I had a real talk with Mum. Stella and I had just moved to Bramble, and after service one Sunday I hung around awhile. Mum said, "So, what's your story, little sister?" We sat here on these steps and I poured out the whole thing. Billy Havisham and the hot-air balloon, the poems, the cordials, Stella being scared, the red trunks and moving—about how all I wished for was a father.

Mum said, "Wishing is good, Willa. But don't ignore today. Every second is precious. Sometimes we aren't even wishing for the thing we really need. You might be looking for beach glass and miss a pretty stone. You might be waiting for that thing you always wanted, when that thing you always needed is staring you in the face."

I was so hopeful back then.

Not today. Today's a different story. Mum hands me a tissue. I blow my nose. "They're perfect for each other, Mum. Sam would make Mother so happy she'd forget to be afraid, and he would be a wonderful father and we could stay in Bramble forever."

Mum doesn't jump in right away. I love that about her. I think it takes a really special person not to jump in right away. Like what you just said was important and it deserves a minute or two. We just sit there watching the birds.

"It's hard to let go of the hurt, Willa," Mum finally says, shaking her head. "When a person's been hurt like your mother was hurt, when your heart's been broken like her heart was broken, but then somehow, some way, you find the courage to stand back up again, well, I think that at that very moment you say to yourself, 'No, no, no, no, NO, never again, uh—uh—uh, NEVER will I let anyone or anything hurt me like that again, and I sure won't let anyone or anything hurt my baby girl.'"

Mum says "baby girl" softly, like a lullaby. I can barely speak.

"But no one is hurting her, Mum. The only one who's hurting anybody is Mother. She's hurting me and she's hurting Sam, and most of all she's hurting herself."

"That's right, honey. And there's not a thing you or I or anybody can do about it until she's ready to remember."

"Remember what, Mum?"

"The love, little sister. The love."

I decide to give Tina another chance and stop by her house on the way home.

"It was Joey Kennelly," she says.

"What?" I'm confused.

"Mother ran into Joey's parents at the Flying Bridge the night before Duke and Dora's wedding. I guess Joey asked his mother if she ever heard of *Forever Young,* and it just happens to be her favorite show. Joey said that you said that Duke and Dora were getting married on Popponesset Beach and that your mother was running the thing, and well, Joey's father's best friend is an editor at the *Cape Cod Times* and . . ."

"I'm sorry, Tina. I'm sorry I blamed you. I completely forgot about JFK. It doesn't matter now anyway. It was all too good to be true. Mother says we're leaving."

"No way!" Tina is mad. "We've got to stop her. She can't ruin your life like that. And mine. I don't want to lose the best friend I've ever had. . . ."

Best friend. "Really, Tina? I'm your best friend?" My heart is breaking.

When I get home, the red trunks are lined up in the front hall and there's a map of Maine on the table.

CHAPTER 26

Simple Gifts

Sometimes we aren't even wishing for the thing we really need.

—Sulamina Mum

The next morning I get up early and bike to the beach. I walk along the water for hours. When I get home, I hear Sam's voice inside as soon as I open our front door.

"What, Stella, what? I don't understand. It's awful about the wedding. You have every right to be upset and everyone feels horrible. But what's that got to do with you and me? Why are you shutting me out? Let me help. I love you, Stella, and I thought that you loved . . ."

Stella storms into the hallway and I lean back against the door to block her. "Willafred." She looks at me disgustedly. "What are you doing?

Spying on me? Haven't you done enough? Please, get out of my way. I'm late for my attorney. . . ."

"Mother, wait!" I plead, but she's already down the steps and in her car.

Sam joins me out on the porch.

"I'm sorry, Sam. It's not you. She's mad at me, not you."

"You have nothing to be sorry about, Willa. Your mother is the grown-up."

When Sam leaves, I throw myself down on my bed and cry. I'm so angry at Stella. I go and pick up the map on the table and shred it into pieces. Then I gather up all the news stories about Duke and Dora's wedding and throw them in the trash.

Later Stella calls. She'll be late. I heat a piece of pizza. I write in my journal, then decide to talk to Sam some more. Maybe we can figure out something together.

It's starting to get dark. I ring Sam's bell. There's no answer. Hopefully he went to find Stella. I walk around to the backyard and stand in front of the labyrinth. I take a deep breath and start to walk.

The grass on the path has been freshly mowed. The flowers are still pretty. It's so quiet all I hear is the sound of my own breathing. In and out. A squirrel crosses in front of me, leaps, and scurries up a tree. A breeze brushes against my face. Happy brown-eyed Susans and their big sisters, the sunflowers, smile at me. Already I feel better.

As I walk a melody comes into my mind. *'Tis a gift to be simple, 'tis a gift to be free. . . .* We sing it at BUC. I begin humming and then sing, "'Tis a gift to be simple, 'tis a gift to be free, 'tis a gift to come down where we ought to be. And when we find ourselves in the place just right . . ."

The song makes me cry and I stop singing. Bramble is the place that's right for me. Pure and simple. Oh, please, Mother, don't make us move again.

I walk toward the center, weaving out, then in, following the old path, one circle after another, looping closer in, then away . . . until finally I reach the center and sit.

By the bench is a frilly purple bush, buddleia, I think Sam called it, the butterfly bush. The petals are soft. It smells like lilacs. My heart's beating fast. I take a deep breath. After a while I feel better.

This place is so peaceful, no wonder Sam looks happy sitting here. Sam, wonderful Sam. *Please, God, please. All I've ever wanted is a father. Please make Stella see how much Sam loves her. . . .*

Later, when I open my eyes, I look over toward my house and I see Mother's face in the study window for one brief moment before she draws the curtains closed. I pluck a sprig of the butterfly bush as a peace offering. I remember how she loved that simple bouquet Sam brought as a gift to the Memorial Day picnic.

When I get home, there's a paper on the table. Flight schedules from Boston to Portland, Maine.

Mother's door is closed, but I know she's awake. As I walk toward her with my peace offering, the light under the door goes out.

I put the butterfly flower in a cup of water and set it on my dresser. I pick up Father's picture. Billy Havisham was famous for his big ideas. That's what I need right now. I lie awake for hours thinking about what Mum said. Trying not to hate Stella so much. I know how hurt Mother is inside and how scared she is to love, but I can't sit by and let her ruin everything, just when we've finally come so close.

Later, before I fall asleep, I remember something Sam once said about how sometimes just a "few quiet words strung together just right can change a person's life."

I get out of bed, pop a cordial in my mouth for good luck, grab my flashlight, and head downstairs and outside. Sam's front-porch door is open. It takes a while in the dark, but I find the letters that I need.

CHAPTER 27

Off Cape

Nobody sees a flower—really it is so small—
we haven't time—and to see takes time.

—Georgia O'Keeffe

"How can she be so cruel?" Tina said. "Doesn't she care about your feelings? You belong here in Bramble. She can't just rip up your roots like some old weed."

It all happened so quickly it still doesn't seem real. I feel like Alice in Wonderland when she fell down that hole. One moment you're fine. The next moment your whole world's turned upside down.

Looking out at the cotton-puff clouds, my forehead pressed against the window over the wing, I replay the final scenes of my movie over and over. The faces and voices of my friends in Bramble. Exactly what each one said before we left. After

Mother read those quiet words, STELLA, WILL YOU MARRY ME? on the Poet's Bramble Board.

We're going to Bermuda for a long weekend before we go to Maine. I'm in no mood for a vacation. Stella's asleep, and as her head nods closer and closer, about to land on my shoulder, I pull my arm away. I'm so angry I can't even look at her. I'm afraid I'll start screaming "I hate you" again and frighten the other passengers.

The sky is blue, but not blue like the sea. I close my eyes back to the movie. Nana wouldn't speak to Stella, she was so mad. Nana gave me a stack of postcards, three pens, a roll of stamps, and a big box of cherry cordials. "You write me as soon as you get there, honey, and I'll send you a box every week, the very best ones just the way you like them, with the pits in for luck. And I'm going to send you all my new taffy flavors so you can rate them for me. And don't forget, Alexander and I want you to help plan our wedding, okay?" When Nana hugged me, Scamp ran crazy circles around us, barking, *What's wrong, what's wrong, what's wrong?*

At Bramblebriar Books, Muffles stared while Mr. Tweed wiped his nose with a handkerchief, then handed me two presents. The first was a book. *Wit and Wisdom of Famous American Women.* "Take a look at that quote by Georgia O'Keeffe," he said. "The one about seeing."

The second gift was a brown leather journal with a yellow sunflower embossed on the cover. Inside Mr. Tweed had written: "To my kindred spirit, Willa Havisham. Remember to keep reading the best books while you are young, like Thoreau said. And then someday, Willa, when you write your own, as I am certain you will, remember what Jo learns in *Little Women.* The secret is to write the truth and put your heart into it. Fondly, Alexander Tweed." I hugged my friend quickly and ran out the door. When I turned back to look, Muffles was staring out at me with those big green eyes, her pink nose pressed against the pane. *Good-bye.*

The plane sinks down a bit and the crackling intercom interrupts my movie. "Good afternoon again, ladies and gentlemen," the pilot announces in a chummy voice, "we're about ten minutes from Hamilton, folks. It's seventy-three degrees and partly sunny. We anticipate a smooth landing. Attendants, please prepare the cabin."

I close my eyes again. Ruby Sivler seemed

genuinely sad. "Sorry you have to move, Willa. My sister, Wanda, wanted your mother to plan her wedding. It's going to be soooo glam. Good luck and call us. Tina and I will miss you."

Sulamina Mum said, "Just remember you've got the love, little sister. That's all anybody ever needs for a miracle. Love keeps working even when you can't see it."

And then, of course, there was Sam. After a big, emotional scene with Mother over the message I wrote on the Bramble Board, Sam stormed out of our house, got on his bike, and took off. We left so early for the airport I never even got to say good-bye.

I did get up the nerve to say good-bye to JFK.

"See ya around, Willa," he said. "Keep in touch."

Big deal. Whoop-de-do. It's not that great of a dimple anyway.

I open the *Wit and Wisdom* book to the Georgia O'Keeffe quote. "Nobody sees a flower—really it is so small—we haven't time. . . ." My eyes fill up again. We had flowers all around us in Bramble, and Stella had all the time in the world.

CHAPTER 28

Lost in the Labyrinth

*Begin at the beginning . . . and go on till you come
to the end: then stop.*

—Lewis Carroll, *Alice's Adventures in Wonderland*

"The girl across the street seems nice," Stella
says, cheerful as a chickadee. I stare through her
like she's an evil figment of my imagination, then
turn back out the kitchen window, lost in my
thoughts, missing every single thing about the sea.

It's a cold, gray January day, but Stella is posi-
tively sunny. Remarkably, just a few months after
leaving the Cape, without shedding a tear or looking back over the bridge, Stella has settled us here
in Portsmouth, Maine, walking distance to a private school with reams of rules, and a short drive
to Stella's job at an investment company.

There she is, sipping black coffee, scouring the

stock market. Stella the Invincible. The cat with nineteen lives. Was Bramble a dream? Did I make the whole thing up?

I slam my bedroom door so hard the windows rattle. I throw myself on the bed, pick up my pen, and scratch how much I hate her into my journal. Then I reach under my pillow for my letters.

Tina misses me so much she "can't eat or sleep." School is boring, as usual. She wants to visit SOON. Thankfully, she doesn't mention Ruby.

Mum says she knows how sad I am, but to keep remembering the love.

Nana and Mr. Tweed seem to be managing just fine without me. They came to visit over the holidays and took me out for lunch. Stella wasn't invited. We discussed wedding plans. They're getting married on Valentine's Day.

Nana said Sam felt awful when he saw the FOR SALE sign on our front door. She gave him our new address. Sam's letters to me are short and pleasant, mostly questions about my new school. He doesn't ask the big question: Why did Stella run away?

I've sent Sam three postcards now, asking about the labyrinth and the Bramble Board and what the eighth graders are reading. When he mentioned

The Old Man and the Sea, by Ernest Hemingway, I bought a copy on the way home from school and finished it that night. It's a nice little book. I copied a line in my journal about the old man's eyes being blue as the sea, "cheerful and undefeated," although right now I can't relate to the "cheerful and unde- feated" part. I miss Bramble. I miss my beach. I am not cheerful.

Sam wrote Stella four letters that I know of, but she ripped them up unopened. Too scared to read the words. I tried piecing one of the letters together out of the trash, but the paper was wet with coffee grounds.

My thirteenth birthday is Friday. The day I looked forward to with such high hopes back when I believed in impossible things. I pull the perfect-looking Portsmouth Prep calendar from my wall and throw the smiling, preppy faces in matching preppy navy sweaters on the floor. No. I won't "try and make the best of it." I won't try to find the purple. I won't be nice to the snooty girl across the street so maybe she'll let me into her club. I won't make it easy for Stella.

I was so foolish to think Bramble would be dif- ferent. Didn't Mother see how happy I was? How people loved us? How we belonged? I was so busy wishing for a father that I forgot the biggest rule of all: Stella makes all the rules.

Mother has business in Bangor on Friday, so she takes me out for an early birthday dinner Wednesday night. She said I could invite Tina last weekend, but the weather was bad and Mrs. Belle was worried about driving. "We'll celebrate when you come for your grandmother's wedding in February," Tina said. "I'll throw an awesome party for you at my house, and I'll invite JFK, okay?"

Before we leave for the restaurant, Mother gives me my birthday presents. A new desk lamp and two monogrammed Portsmouth Prep sweaters.

Stella orders for us: Caesar salad, shrimp cocktail, steak, and baked potatoes. I pick at the food.

I try to be civil, but when the waiter brings out the cake with thirteen candles, and he and Stella start singing, "Happy birthday to you . . . ," and then those strangers at the next table join in, and when they get to the "dear . . ." part, they pause and Stella shouts, "Willafred," and then she smiles and says, "Make a wish," I think I will vomit. I pick up the knife and stare at Stella with my eyes wide open. I will never wish again.

That night I lie in bed feeling all alone in the world. *What am I going to do?* I open up the new journal Mr. Tweed gave me. "The secret is to write the truth and put your heart into it." I slam the book shut and cry myself to sleep.

I dream about the labyrinth. I'm lost and I'm circling, around and around. I don't know how to get back to the beginning. I wake up sweating. My heart is pounding. I know what I have to do.

CHAPTER 29

Friday the Thirteenth

*And so when I couldn't stand it no longer I
lit out.*

—Mark Twain, *The Adventures of Huckleberry Finn*

It's the morning of my thirteenth birthday.
Friday the thirteenth. *Happy birthday to me, happy
birthday to me . . .*

I told Stella I was sick this morning just as she
was leaving for her business meeting in Bangor. She
couldn't force me to go to school sick, especially on
my birthday, so she said, "Stay in bed and drink lots
of fluids. I'll ask Mrs. Hickey to look in on you." Mrs.
Hickey is the nice retired nurse who lives next door.

As soon as Stella's car leaves the driveway, I get
dressed and put on my coat. On Stella's bed I set
up the little wooden easel I bought at the art store.
I place my letter on it, with the candy underneath.

Dear Mother,

I hope you like the cordials. I know Father used to send them to you. I know about the heart-shaped trunk. I know about the poems. I know why you're so afraid.

I'm sorry I ruined your business, Mother. You were a wonderful wedding planner. But your weddings were missing something.

Go ahead and try a cordial. Take the pit in your hand and look at it. I know it's small and ugly now, but if you plant it and water it, give it sunshine and space for roots, someday that seed will blossom.

That's why Father sent you those cordials and poems every week. And even though it was a foolish idea, that's why he planned to pick you up in Poet's Park and whisk you off in a balloon the day after your wedding. He did it because he loved you.

That's the thirteenth secret ingredient.

Love.

You can get away with wilted flowers or a wrinkled dress. Those twelve ingredients you so perfectly planned.

You were right, Mother. They all matter so much on that one fairy-tale day.

The next day, all that matters is the love.

Yours truly,
Willafred Havisham
The Wedding Planner's Daughter

CHAPTER 30

Home at Last

Who has seen the wind?
Neither you nor I:
But when the trees bow down their heads,
The wind is passing by.

—Christina Georgina Rossetti, "Who Has Seen the Wind?"

I had to switch buses three times, but when I saw that silver roller-coaster bridge, it was worth the trip. I pushed up the window and the wind whooshed in, laughing like it had been waiting. *Welcome, Willa, welcome home.*

In Falmouth I found a taxi place and gave the driver my destination.

The old Gracemore estate looks deserted when we pull up in front. All the shades are down. I pay the driver and stand on the street for a minute. Then I walk around back. The labyrinth looks lonely. It hasn't been cared for in a while. There are mounds of leaves, scattered sticks, dead flower vines and stalks, weeds never cleared from last season. They will block the sun from the sprouts underneath in the spring. A bright red cardinal flies in and out again. The feeders are empty.

I enter the labyrinth and begin walking. Circling slowly toward the center. When I reach the bench, I close my eyes and take a deep breath. It's January, but I'm not cold. It's always warmer by the sea.

I start thinking back over this past year. How much I loved living here in Bramble. How I felt like I belonged for the very first time. Nana, Tina, Sam, Mum, Mr. Tweed—all the people who love me here, they all flash through my mind.

I think about my first date, the movie with JFK. How he held my hand. Our walk on the beach. My first kiss.

On and on I remember. I sit on this bench with my eyes closed, waiting. Like Stella in Poet's Park. I am waiting for someone to come.

I wonder what Father would look like now, thirteen years older than the picture on my dresser? I bet he'd laugh when he saw my eyes, the same dark blue as his, "sparkling like the sea on a sunny summer day." He'd scoop me in his arms and twirl me around just like I always imagined. "There's my girl," he'd say, laughing. But no, this is now.

I picture the Poet coming to get me. Except the Poet is a person, Sam Gracemore. A man with a sad past. A man who thought he had a chance at happiness again with Mother. Sam would smile when he saw me sitting here. That beautiful smile that could melt Alaska. He'd say, "Willa, hello, fancy meeting you here."

But no, I'm not waiting for Sam.

As I sit here with my eyes still closed, longer and longer, starting to get chilly, I imagine Tina walking into the backyard and finding me. She'd be so excited. "What are you doing out here?" she'd shout. "You'll freeze to death. Come on, let's go."

Then I picture Nana. "Give me a hug, shmug."

Mr. Tweed . . . Sulamina Mum . . . I'd be so happy to see them all, and yet . . .

"Willafred." I hear my name. And for the first time it sounds beautiful. I've been sitting here in the garden so long I know I must be dreaming.

"Willafred."

The voice is familiar, but different.

"Willafred!"

I open my eyes.

It's Mother. She's running toward me shouting loudly, but in a gentle voice, "Willafred, what were you thinking of?" stumbling over branches, "running off like that," falling on the slippery ground, "are you okay? I was worried sick. . . ." closer and closer, around and around, nearer, then farther away, through the labyrinth, Mother is crying and running faster now, "Thank God I found you, Willafred," stumbling again, "I'm sorry for hurting you. I'm sorry I took you away from Bramble. . . ." Sobbing, Mother leaps over the last hedge, throws her arms around me, and this is not a dream.

And then, for the first time in my life, my mother looks at me, stares deep into my eyes . . . and really *looks* at me. She takes my face in her hands and looks in my eyes like I'm the one and only thing that makes her happiest in the world.

"I love you, Willa," she says.

My mother called me *Willa*.

"Happy birthday, Willa. I love you so much."

"I love you too, Mom. I always have."

Mother hugs me, and we rock back and forth in that circle. I can feel her heart beating against mine. Tiny snowflakes melt into the tears on our cheeks and we begin to laugh. We stay here like this for a long time, neither one wanting to go.

Then, like lightning, it strikes me. All those years, all those birthdays, wishing for a father, thinking that's what I wanted most in the world. I was wrong. That wasn't it.

What I wanted, what I needed most, was my mother. To really, truly see me.

CHAPTER 31

The Wedding Planner's Daughter

"I don't want a fashionable wedding, but only those about me whom I love. . . ."
So she made her wedding gown herself, sewing into it the tender hopes . . . of a girlish heart.

—Louisa May Alcott, *Little Women*

Something old, something new, something borrowed, something blue, and a lucky sixpence . . . Nana says, "I've got something old, *me*, and something new, *Tweed*." She borrows Stella's satin wedding purse, says, "Who needs blue when we've got the sea?" and then asks me to sew a cherry pit in the hem of her dress for luck.

Nana made the dress herself, pale purple chiffon, nothing fancy, but beautiful.

Mr. Tweed is wearing a gray pin-striped suit, purple bow tie, and a sprig of lavender for a boutonniere. New brother and sister Scamp and Muffles look adorable in their matching purple polka-dot bows.

Tina and I are wearing our June Bug dresses. Mine feels snug across the chest.

Tina helped me sew sachet pillows of lavender, Nana's favorite scent, as favors for the wedding guests. We got the lavender from the labyrinth.

"Good thing about lavender," Sam says, "it blooms again and again."

Nana doesn't know it yet, but Tina and I also tied up little cellophane bags of purple taffy, Brambleberry, and hid a Swedish fish in each one for the fun of it.

Mr. Tweed and I had a hard time, but we finally agreed on some readings from our very favorite authors. Sulamina Mum said to "leave the Bible part" to her. You should have seen Mum when she first saw me and Mother back home. She came flying down Main Street like some crazy peacock and swooped us both right off the ground.

I'm keeping the Sixth Ingredient simple. Yellow carnations. Tina and I strung fairy lights around the archway entrance to BUC and lit tall candles in the windows, but that's the extent of the glamour. Nana and Mr. Tweed said they wanted simple.

The organist begins, and the bride and groom enter together. "Nobody's giving anybody away," Nana said. They walk slowly, arm in arm, nodding at each guest.

I look over at Mother and Sam. Mother is glowing. She's smiling and crying, her head on Sam's shoulder. Tina sees them too and flips her hair back, case closed.

At my cue Mrs. Bellimo belts it out.

After the ceremony we head to Bramblebriar Books for dinner. Mother and Sam each give a toast. Mum says a prayer. The first course is Alexander's favorite, chowda made from Nana's secret recipe.

Nana and Alexander dance the night away. Their happiness floats about like fairy dust, gently coating every heart in the room.

Mother and Sam dance every dance too, except for the one Sam dances with me. "May I have this dance, young lady?" he says with a bow.

"Why yes, kind sir, I'd be delighted."

It is the first time I have ever danced at a wedding, but Sam knows what he is doing. He sweeps me around the room like a princess, and I never once step on his toes.

That night I replay the wonderful movie again and again in my mind. Mother knocks at my door and I invite her in.

She sits down on the bed. "It was a beautiful wedding, Willa. Congratulations."

"Well, I had the best teacher ever. I am the wedding planner's daughter, after all."

Mother's eyes fill with tears. I reach out to touch her cheek.

"Don't worry, Mother, I have no intention of making a career out of this."

"I know, Willa," she says with a laugh. "It's just, I'm so proud of you."

"Thanks, Mother. Weddings are fun, and I'd like to plan my own someday, but I have great expectations for my future. Just like you always taught me. I don't think weddings are my real talent anyway. I think I'd rather write about them. Maybe I'll be a writer someday."

"I know you will, Willa." Mother hugs me. "And I'll be your biggest fan."

CHAPTER 32

Miracles

*Where there is great love there are always
miracles.*

—**Willa Sibert Cather**

So that's my story. Number thirteen was lucky
after all. The weekend after Nana's wedding Stella
and Sam eloped to Nantucket and my impossible
dream finally came true.

Mother left me a note on my pillow.

Dear Willa,
You were right. It's not about the big wedding day.
It's the days that come after that count. We can't
wait to share them with you.
Love,
Mom and Sam

When they got back from their honeymoon, Mother and I moved into Sam's house. After several long family discussions we decided to dust off the chandeliers, set out the wicker chairs, and reopen the once famous Bramblebriar Inn.

Mother hired the interior decorators and oversaw the renovation. Sam (he says to call him Dad only if and when I want to, but I'm kind of used to "Sam," so that's good for now) and I worked on the labyrinth together. We added new flowers and birdhouses. Now the tourist guides say we're one of the "grandest hotels" on Cape.

I'm done adding secret ingredients to wedding gowns, but I did sow one last cherry seed. Right in my new front yard. Someday it will grow into a cherry tree with blossoms sweet as perfume.

The red trunks are gone for good, but there is a new statue by the labyrinth. It's the present Mother and Sam gave me after their honeymoon: a girl with a long ponytail, stretched out on her stomach on the grass, smiling as she reads a book.

Mother and Sam love being innkeepers. Stella runs the house and pays the bills. Occasionally she'll agree to plan a wedding at the inn, just for the fun of it, and she lets me and Tina help. Sam's in charge of the kitchen and grounds. I look after the library.

I just found a book by Willa Cather. I can tell by her name we'll be kindred spirits.

Oh, and I write the Bramble Board now. Mother's grown used to the idea. The travel books call it "Bramble's favorite conversation piece." Stella says it's good for business. When Sulamina Mum saw the Cather quote about love and miracles, she laughed out loud. "Mmm-mmm, little sister, got that right."

Nana and Grandfather Tweed combined their businesses a few months back. Now they are Sweet Bramble Books. They took first place in both the Best Sweets and the Best Bookstore categories for the Upper Cape in *Cape Cod Life*. Finally Nana won with a taffy called Cherry Cordial.

Tina and I are still best friends, and I decided Ruby's not so bad after all. She found a great new hairstyle for me, and I now have a greater appreciation for her talents.

JFK seemed happy to see me back. Dimple cute as ever. No more walks on the beach yet, but we've got lots of time.

I bike to the beach almost every day. I walk

along looking for beach glass and jingle shells, then I sit on the jetty and smile out at the sea.

Mum always says the only prayer you ever need is just two words.

I've said "thank you" so often now it must be written on my heart.

Well, that's all for now. We still have rules, and I've got homework. When you visit Cape Cod, stop by Bramble. I'll show you where to find the sweetest books in town.

Until then, have great expectations. Keep believing your dreams will come true.

And remember, when life throws you a pit . . . plant a cherry tree.

Willa's Pix—Recommended by Willa Havisham

The Adventures of Huckleberry Finn, Mark Twain
The Adventures of Tom Sawyer, Mark Twain
Alice's Adventures in Wonderland, Lewis Carroll
Anne of Green Gables, Lucy Maud Montgomery
Charlotte's Web, E. B. White
The Diary of a Young Girl, Anne Frank
Great Expectations, Charles Dickens
Little House in the Big Woods, Laura Ingalls Wilder
Little Women, Louisa May Alcott
Matilda, Roald Dahl
The Member of the Wedding, Carson McCullers
The Old Man and the Sea, Ernest Hemingway
Sarah, Plain and Tall, Patricia MacLachlan
The Secret Garden, Frances Hodgson Burnett
Through the Looking-Glass, Lewis Carroll

And the works of Emily Dickinson, Christina
Georgina Rossetti, Robert Frost, Henry David
Thoreau, Walt Whitman, and William Shakespeare.

Acknowledgments

I am grateful to so many people for the love and support that enable me to do the work that gives me such joy. First off, thank you to Simon & Schuster editor Alyssa Eisner, who opened the castle door of children's publishing and let me in the club. Throughout the give and take of revisions for our first picture book, *How Prudence Proovit Proved the Truth About Fairy Tales,* Alyssa encouraged me to write a middle-grade novel. I had my mind set on more picture books. Alyssa kept asking, "So what about a novel?" Then one evening, relaxing after a Society of Children's Book Writers and Illustrator's Conference (fabulous organization) in Philadelphia, Alyssa said, "Let me throw a title out at you: *The Wedding Planner's Daughter.*" That's all she said. Just the title. My initial reaction was that it was too commercial for me, but I wrote it down and proceeded to pitch more picture book ideas.

Then, as I was driving home to Albany the next morning, I felt the presence of Miss Havisham from *Great Expectations* in the backseat. In that moment I thought, wow, if I can make this book fun and literary, too, that's exciting. A few miles later, Willa came into my mind, and I felt in my heart how desperately she wanted a father, and then Willa's mother, Stella, appeared, and then Nana Clancy, Mr. Tweed and Bramble . . . and I furiously filled two yellow tablets with notes on my steering wheel (definitely not recommended) as I drove home. Thank you, Alyssa, for your magical wisdom, your great kindness, and your indefatigable enthusiasm.

Thanks also to Brenda Bowen, Elizabeth Law, Katrina Groover, Greg Stadnyk, Chava Wolin, Kevin Lewis, Tracey van Straaten, Mark Siegel, Emily Thomas, Annie Kelly, Alexandra Lambert, Katie McGarry, Michelle Montague, Erica Stahler, and everyone at Simon & Schuster Books for Young Readers. Thanks also to my wonderful agent, Tracey Adams, Adams Literary, for your calm presence and superb advice. I am so grateful to the friends who critique my work in WOW (Writers on Wednesday), Tuesday Muse, and Food for Thought, including the talented children's writers: Jennifer Groff, Nancy Castaldo, Debbi Michiko Florence, Jacqueline Rogers, Kyra Teis

Zonderman, Lois Feister Huey, Rose Marie Kent, Liza Frenette, Barbara Wood, Karen Beil, Lynn Blankman and Ellen Laird. Thanks also to children's writer friends Theresa Rae, Karen Pandell, Ann Burg, Daniel Mahoney, Teri Daniels, Phil Teibolt, Cheri Hinchman Widzowski, Cathy Gio, Joan Krege, Eric Luper, Patricia Williams, Julie Winkler, Lisa Rowe Fraustino, and Laurie Krauss Kiernan.

And, for those precious early words of encouragement, thanks to authors Carla Neggers, Laurie Halse Anderson, Kay Winters, Pamela Jane, editors Judy O'Malley, Anita Silvey, and publishing marvel Barb Burg. I appreciate the research assistance from Margaret Garrett and Tom Barnes at the Guilderland Public Library, and the welcome cheers from the Youth Services Department—Leslie, Barbara, Julia, Cherry, Terry, and Suzanne—you are the sort of children's librarians every child deserves. Thanks to Darryl Davis and the West Mountain Inn, Arlington, Vermont, for the labyrinth inspiration. Thanks to Diane Walshhampton, Donna Amato, Jo-Ann Gejay, Alana Lucia, Linda Triplett, Emily Spooner, Colleen Mickle, Deb Wein, Meg Seinberg-Hughes (librarian extraordinaire), Stacey

Kirk, Kathy O'Boyski-Butler, Charlene Dare, Lauren Gay, Tara Molloy-Grocki, and Eileen Bray, and all of my friends at Guilderland Elementary School, a place of legendary learning and love.

Thanks to Susan Novotny, Kim Soyka, and Rachel King of The Book House and The Little Book House, Stuyvesant Plaza, Albany, New York; to Frank Hodge, Hodge-Podge Books, Albany; Janet Hutchison, The Open Door Bookstore, Schenectady; to Carol Chittenden, Eight Cousins Bookstore, Falmouth, Cape Cod; and posthumously to Denise McCoy of the Bookmark, Loudonville, New York. Thank you to my friends Kathy Johnson, Ellen Donovan, and Paula Davenport (the Ya-Yas); Susan and Bruce Carlson; Pauline and Fred Miller; Carla Neggers and Joe Jewel; Kathi and Dave Shamlian; Lois and Jon Pasternack; Janet and Ned Trombly; Gail and Mike Moran; Bill and Mary Kahl, Joe Curtin, Lori Goodale, Mary Jane and Ken Reilly; Lisa Burianek and John Cropley; Jan Cioffi, Eileen Burton, Libby Mahoney, Sheila Murphy, Gladys Craig, Sybille Colby, Joan and Joe Scotti; Janice and Larry Stevens; Judy and Steve LeGraw; Mary Grace and Dennis Tompkins; Frank Scanlon; Amy Van

Amburgh; Gail George; Judy Calogero; Meg and Scott Bassinson; Kerry and Wayne Castronovo; Kathy and Charlie Jordan; Jean Claude and Anne-Marie Simille; Regina and Scott Keenholts; Lynne, Kathy and Mary Mahoney; Addie Muhlfelder, Joan Noonan, Hania Stowowy; Hilarie Tongue; Ann and Cosimo Crupi; Joanne Pisarski; Judy Conlen; Ellen and Kevin Snyder; Kate and Frank Sorrentino; Kellie Fox and Tom Fox; Bonnie Nunziato; Kristen Zadrozinski, Cookie McInness, Gail DiBattista, Betty Stefos, Wendy Alexopoulus, Doris O'Neil, Jan Bosse, Linda Crescenzi, and Marge and Jack McNulty; and childhood friends Sue "P", Sue "T", Mary "H", Mary "M", Kathy, Theresa, Maureen, Denise, and Jean; to Gloria and Bill Malone, for the key to my Cape Cod dream; and to neighbors Claire and Chris Kondochristie, Lynn and Ray Butti, Cookie and Don McInness, Ginny and Frank Lammer, Fran Risko, and Rowena Lammer for answering countless Cape Cod questions.

With deepest gratitude to my mother, gifted poet Peg Spain Murtagh; my father-in-law Tony and Sadie Paratore; my kindred-artist brother Jerry; my amazing sister, Noreen, and Mike, Ryan, and Jack; my wonderful brothers Michael, and Donnie Reznek; Danny, and Liane Terrio; and to Kevin and Colleen, Liam, Lauren, and Brendan; to my brother-in-law Jim and to Maryann; Carmen, and Aunt Mary, Aunt Mimi, and Aunt Virginia; and to Aunt Jane who gave me *Little Women*; and Nancy Davison who gave me my first blank book.

Finally, and most importantly, to my husband, Tony, and to our three beautiful sons, Connor, Dylan, Christopher. I am so lucky to share this wonderful life with you.

C.M.P. April 2004